*Diamond*Stone Productions Presents

DAMAGED GOODS

By: Nikki Urban
The Princess of Urban Erotica

Cover and Graphics: Carrissa Glanton @
Diamond Eyez Designs
Model: Quazavia Gantt
ISBN: 0615474128
ISBN: 9780615474120
First Edition
First Printing November 2010
DiamondStone Productions Presents
Jacksonville, FL 32211
Printed in the United States of America

Acknowledgements

First and foremost I have to thank God. It's through him that I can do all things!! I have to thank my husband for standing by my as I pursue my dream. I want to thank my parents... I love you JoJo and dad. To my God-father... I love you so much.

To my manager Q, you keep me on my "A" game.

To the Clique.... Y'all know who you ladies are!!! I LOVE YOU ALL SO MUCH!! YOU ARE ALL THE TRUE DEFINITION OF TRUE FRIENDS!!!

To all of the independent Black bookstores...there is a need for you! You help authors like me have an opportunity to share our work with the masses....

To the fans, readers, and book clubs... I THANK YOU SO MUCH FOR ALL OF YOUR SUPPORT AND LOVE!! WITHOUT YOU THERE IS NO ME... REAL TALK!!!

NIKKI URBAN
The Princess of Urban Erotica...

Nikki Urban Wants to Hear From YOU!!!

Call NIKKI URBAN and tell her what you think about the book…

904.469.6353

Prologue

Russell was excited because his baby-girl was turning sixteen. He had been raising Vasthai since she was born. In 1970, when his daughter was born it was taboo for interracial dating. Russell was born in the south in 1954. He saw first-hand what happened to black men and he knew not a lot had changed when he turned sixteen in 1970.

Russell was a handsome dark chocolate man, with gray eyes and a smile that would make any woman want to be in his bed. He had fallen in love with a Japanese woman named Kaori.

In December of 1969, Russell and Kaori laid together for the first time and in September of 1970, he became a father. His child's mother left him never to return again. Russell and his mother were left to raise Vasthai.

When Vasthai was two, Russell gathered his mother and his child; and left his home for a better life. Once in the new city, Russell learned the trade of mechanics and was able to save enough money to open his own garage.

He was able to provide a good life for his daughter. He spoiled her with whatever she wanted. She was his "princess" and he doted on her with his love and affection. Russell always made sure Vasthai was in the latest fashions, and that her hair was always done. Now, sixteen years later he had watched his daughter turn into a beautiful young woman entering womanhood.

Russell was planning a surprise party for Vasthai for the weekend after her birthday and he was getting prepared for Saturday's event. Little did he know devastation was heading his way.

Russell ran into the hospitals' emergency area and demanded to see his daughter. The nurse rushed from behind the nurse's station and tried to calm the distraught man, "Sir... I am going to have to ask you to take a seat over here in the waiting area." She said.

Russell looked at her as if she was stone crazy. If she thought for one moment that he was going to take a seat while his daughter was in that hospital the Bitch had him fucked up.

"I don't give a good got damn what you want!!! If someone does not come and take me to my daughter I will tear this motherfucker down!! So I suggest you take me to my daughter, because if I don't get some results the shit won't be pretty!!" Russell responded as he walked around the woman and proceeded down the hall.

The black nurse who was also behind the desk walked up behind the angry man and said, "Sir, let me help you. What is your daughter's name?" She asked as she grabbed his hand and looked into his eyes.

Russell had no idea what had happened to his daughter. Today was her sixteen[th] birthday party at the skating rink and all was going good until he realized Vasthai had left the party.

She was his everything and he would lay down his life for his baby or kill anyone who did harm to her. He was suddenly knocked back to

reality when he heard the doctor calling for any relatives of Vasthai Douglas.

"Yeah...Yeah... I'm her father!!! What's going on with my daughter?" He asked the doctor in a scared voice. The doctor and Russell talked as he explained what happened to her.

Russell was led to his daughter's private room. As soon as he saw her, he went to her bed and grabbed her hand. Although, she was physically wounded; she was emotionally and mentally torn.

Vasthai fell into her father's arms and began to cry. She was so ashamed of what had happened to her. As much as Russell tried to console his daughter... in her mind all she saw was the traumatic events that had taken her innocence. From that day forward Vasthai was never the same.

The Letter

Chapter 1

2008

Vasthai pulled up to her house in her 2007 black Mercedes CL S63 AMG. As she pulled up the driveway of her multi-million dollar home, she stopped at the mailbox and got the mail. After retrieving the mail, she continued up the driveway to the house.

Once inside she realized her husband and children were not home from the store. She went to her bedroom to undress. After she put on her Baby Phat jogging suit she sat on the bed and went through the mail. Vasthai sat up straight when she saw that there was a letter addressed to her from her son.

Her oldest son, Tyrone, was locked up doing time for rape. Although, she knew he was guilty of the crime he was accused of, she could not turn her back on him. She had unconditional love for her children. Vasthai looked at the letter and then opened it.

Dear Momma,

I know it has been some time since I have last written you. Here I am almost three years into my twenty year sentence trying to maintain. Everyday I think about the mistakes I have made. I sit in my cell and think to myself... damn I had such

a bright future ahead of me and I fucked that up, because my manhood was bruised.

I miss you, Daddy, Kamron, and Tyson. I would give anything just to see my family. The pictures you all send me help me, but, it's not the same as seeing you in the flesh. Mom, I just want to tell you that I have great remorse for what I did to Shawn. It's ironic that I have had the same pain that I once inflicted on someone else also done to me.

Since the time I have been in prison, I have been fighting to keep from being someone's fuck boy, but every dog does have their day. I was raped by an inmate here in prison. As I was being fucked by the man who wanted my goods, I saw visions of Shawn laying before me crying and taking my penis in her.

It was at that moment that I could feel her pain. I could feel the immense pain and shame that she felt. It was then I knew I was getting my karma for the shit I had done to someone who didn't deserve it.

It's been three years, six months, and twenty-three days since I have been incarcerated. I was nineteen years old when I entered prison. Now I'm a man who is twenty-two years old. I have many regrets in my life and my greatest regret was committing the crime that sent me to prison. Everyday, I replay in my mind, the day I was sentenced.

I was dumb, young, and I couldn't take rejection. Because of my insecurities and stupidity, I fucked up my life, Shawn's life, and the lives of my

*family members as well. When I first entered prison
I had no idea what to expect. I was scared shitless,
but here I am, more than three years later at the
lowest point in my life.*

*It has been over a year since the last time I
saw you. Mom, you are the only person who I want
to see. There are many things that I need to
apologize to you for.*

Love You,
Tyrone

"Hey baby!! What's going on with you?"
He asked. Before Vasthai could answer his question
he saw the letter in her hand. He grabbed the letter
and read it. After he finished reading the letter he
knew exactly why his wife was upset. Patrick knew
his stepson's letter was triggering his wife's
emotions.

Patrick remembered the first time he saw
Vasthai in his hospital. He was instantly struck by
her beauty and he knew he was going to make her
his wife. He was a new medical doctor straight from
Howard University's Medical School and she was
his first patient.

Although, he was nervous about her being
his first patient, Patrick was determined to make
sure that she was going to be in "good hands" with
him.

Patrick grabbed his wife's face in his hand
and leaned in to kiss her lips. "Baby, you have to
tell him the truth. I know this will be hard for you,
but he has to know the truth." He told her.

Vasthai looked at her husband, picked up her cigarette, and inhaled deeply. "I know. I was just thinking about making flight reservations to go see him." She replied as she continued to inhale the smoke from her lit cigarette through her nose.

Vasthai got up from the bed and walked to the window. She looked out of the window reminiscing on her past, the things that had happened to her, and the things she was going to do out of revenge.

Although, her husband knew everything about her; she never told a soul about how she could not let go of the pain from her past. Now she was going to tell her sins to her son.

Three Years Earlier

Chapter 2

"Will the defendant please rise for sentencing." The judge ordered the young man who was on trial for the brutal rape of an eighteen year old high school girl to stand. The trial was well publicized because the crime was extremely gruesome. The man on trial was accused and convicted of abducting a young girl from her house and brutally raping her multiple times in an abandoned building.

"Mr. James, you do understand that you have been convicted of kidnapping, rape, and imprisonment. My job is to impose sentence. Mr. James, your crime is one of the most hideous crimes that have been presented in my courtroom. I have little empathy or compassion for you. My only hope is that you find some redemption while you serve your time in prison." The judge said to the defendant waiting to hear his fate.

Tyrone James was a young man from the right side of the tracks raised by his mother and stepfather in an upper middle-class African-American community. His stepfather was a prominent physician and his mother was a stay at home mother.

He was the eldest of three siblings. His parents did the best they could to offer their

children all of the opportunities that their monetary wealth could muster.

As Tyrone faced his pending sentence, his mother sat two rows behind her son praying for strength. Vasthai was in the courtroom each and everyday showing her support for her son.

Although, she did not condone her son's actions, he was still her son and she loved him unconditionally. The past year of her life was one of continual stress and worry over her oldest child.

She and her husband paid for the one of the best defense lawyers, but Vasthai saw the writing on the wall. The writing on the wall told her that her son, Tyrone, was headed to jail for an indefinite amount of time.

"Young man, I sentence you to the maximum sentence of twenty years in the Mississippi State Penitentiary. Your time is to start immediately. Bailiff, please remove this man from the courtroom." These were the last words Tyrone heard as he was led away in handcuffs to a new world that was unknown to him.

Vasthai got one last glimpse of her son as he was taken away. She could see the tears in his eyes. At that moment, she saw a little scared boy being led away to become a man in a world of men who were habitual criminals.

She stood where she was a little longer before she headed out the door. With a heavy heart and broken spirit, Vasthai walked out the courtroom entering into a world that was incomplete, because her son was no longer physically with her.

Tyrone was taken away and placed in the county jail while he waited for his transport to the Mississippi Prison. He was in isolation because many of the inmates knew he was the perpetrator of the rape of the young girl; who everyone knew as Shawn Doe. The correctional officers were afraid that if he were put in public population he would be found dead in his cell.

Tyrone was in the county jail for three days. He was called from his cell, and taken to his awaiting bus, and was waiting to be driven to his new permanent home. The trip to Mississippi was a twelve hour drive.

The trip for Tyrone was one of fear and anxiety. He slept little and kept a watchful eye on all of the other inmates that were riding with him. Although, he acted as if he was tough and rugged on the outside; the truth was, he was a punk ass boy from a good home that took his fantasy of a girl he wanted too far.

Tyrone was a junior in high school and was headed to Howard University to study law when he started dating Shawn. He always wanted to be her boyfriend, but each time he thought that they would be together she would be in a relationship with someone else. The two of them remained the best of friends and he was always the shoulder of comfort for her whenever she needed it.

Tyrone was one of the most popular boys in his high school and could have had any of the "chicken heads" that were always on his dick, but he wanted Shawn.

When he got the call from her he was shocked. She had found out that her last boyfriend was cheating on her. As he rode to the prison his mind went back to that phone call.

"Hello, may I speak to Tyrone?" A voice of sweet satin spoke through the cell phone. "What's going on with you Shawn?" He asked her as he sat up in his bed. Whenever he got a call from Shawn he made sure she had his undivided attention.

Before the conversation got started Shawn broke down and cried into the phone. Tyrone's heart immediately felt for her and he wanted to rescue her from her misery. "What's wrong Shawn?" He asked again as he got up and started to put on some clothes.

"I found out that Cory has been cheating on me with that trick ass bitch Lisa. He even had the fucking nerve to bring that bitch to the same party that I was at." Her words had sorrow and extreme devastation.

Shawn and Cory had been together since their freshman year. She lost her virginity to him when she turned sixteen, but now she regretted giving him something that she held so close to her.

"Shawn where are you? I'm about to get in my car and come to where you are." He said as he grabbed his car keys and headed for the front door to leave. Shawn was still at the party with her girlfriends. She was trying to keep her friends from stomping the shit out of Lisa.

When Shawn saw her boyfriend walk in the party with another girl on his arm she snapped the fuck off and confronted him! The look on Cory's

face was priceless when he saw Shawn at the party. He knew he was busted and the drama was about to be on.

Shawn walked up to her rival and smacked the dog shit out of her! Before Lisa could strike her back Cory jumped in between them. The venom of a woman's scorn was released from Shawn's mouth. "You punk ass nigga!! How are you going to play me with this tore up bitch! I mean if you are going to cheat bitch, at least upgrade! This trifling bitch doesn't have shit on me!" Shawn was hot and embarrassed. She was a trooper and she was going keep on pushing. She hurried out the door and called the first person that came to her mind-Tyrone.

Tyrone was there to pick her and her girls up within fifteen minutes. After he dropped her friends off the two of them went to the Waffle House and talked. After that night, they were together, finally. They were a couple for two years and even decided to go to Howard together, but the shit fell apart when Shawn wanted to be free to do her own thing.

Tyrone started to see changes in Shawn. He began to question her, but each time he confronted her he got the same bullshit- she loved him and he was the only one. It was not until he ran up on Shawn with another nigga in the mall. He was so enraged by her betrayal that he walked up to them in the mall and started to whip the other dude's ass.

Tyrone caught an assault charge but his stepfather was able to pull some strings and get his record expunged. He was still able to get into Howard. After he saw Shawn, the one girl who he

17

thought he loved with someone else, he was not the same.

It was the summer before Tyrone and Shawn were to head to Howard, when Tyrone started to stalk Shawn. Wherever she was he would magically appear. Until one hot July day he saw Shawn get out of the car with the same boy he saw her with in the mall.

He waited for her to get to her door. Tyrone swiftly ran up behind her placing his hand over her mouth and dragging her into his car. Shawn was screaming and pleading for him not to hurt her. He could see nothing but red when he looked at her.

"Whore! You cheated on me and you didn't expect me to get back at you!" He said as he drove them out into the boonies. Shawn was afraid. She had never seen that deranged look in his eyes before. She said a silent prayer and sat quietly in the car.

They were outside of the city limits when he finally stopped the car and pulled Shawn out by her hair. He saw an abandoned building and they headed inside.

"Lay down!" Tyrone commanded. When Shawn refused Tyrone began to beat her. He beat her until she was semi-conscious. "Look what you made me do! I was good to you and that wasn't good enough for you! You had to go and fuck the next man!" His words were slurred and his face was tormented.

As he demeaned and undressed her Tyrone began to suck her breasts. His dick got hard as he saw her struggling to get free, but he was too strong

for her. He pulled down his pants, pulled out his dick, and pushed his manhood into her. Shawn screamed from the pain. Her pussy was dry and tender. When he realized her pussy was dry he went down to her pussy and started eating her.

Shawn was beaten but she could not control her body. The feel of his tongue made her pussy explode in his face. When Tyrone tasted her pussy juice he looked at her and said, "Just like I thought... you like that shit...don't you bitch!!" Tyrone raped her for several hours. When he was done he left her there naked and beaten.

Tyrone sped off never looking back. All he could see in his mind was Shawn getting out of another man's car. He rationalized his actions by telling himself that Shawn's pussy belonged to him and no other man was going to fuck her but him.

He pulled into the parking lot of his boy Darius' apartment complex. Tyrone got out of the car, ran up the two flights of stairs, and started beating on the door. Darius opened the door and Tyrone pushed past him.

"What the fuck is up with you Tyrone!? You know you interrupting me from getting my dick sucked! This better be important!" Darius said to his friend as he went to his bedroom and closed the door from the prying ears of his awaiting company.

Tyrone looked at his oldest friend and could see the concern in his eyes. He went over to the bar and poured a shot of Patrone.

Darius sat on the couch and waited for Tyrone to say something. "I fucked up! I'm in trouble and I know it!" He said.

"What are you talking about?" Darius asked as he walked over to the bar and poured another drink for himself. "I saw Shawn get out of another man's car and I just snapped. I pulled her into my car. Drove her out into the middle of nowhere and fucked her senseless. After I was done I left her there."

Darius closed his eyes, because his ears couldn't believe what they were hearing. He was hearing one of his oldest friends tell him that he just kidnapped his ex-girlfriend, raped her, and left her God knows where. Darius knew Tyrone was upset when Shawn told him it was over, but he never in a million years thought he would do some shit like this.

"What the fuck do you mean that you pulled Shawn into your car, drove out somewhere, and fucked her!! Nigga do you hear what you are saying!!!? You are saying that you kidnapped your ex, raped her, and left her!" Darius was perplexed. He had no idea how to help him, but what he did know was that he was not about to get involved with his bullshit.

"Where did you leave her Tyrone?" Darius asked. "I took her out to that old abandoned building out past route one." Tyrone said as he sat down.

"Look, Tyrone, you and I have been friends since for forever, but on this shit, I don't know how to help you. The best thing I can tell you to do, is tell your parents to get you the best defense lawyer that they can find, because you are about to need

one!" Darius told his friend as he went to his room and put on his socks and shoes.

Tyrone knew his friend was right. He was fucked and he was going down. He finished the last of his drink and headed for the door to leave.

When Darius returned to the living room he found it empty. "Destiny, get dressed. I need for you to ride with me somewhere." Darius called to his girl in the other room. As he waited for her to get dressed he prayed that Shawn was alive when he got to her. They rode to where Shawn was in silence.

Darius and Destiny arrived at the abandoned building where Shawn was just as she was regaining consciousness. She looked like hell and Darius could not believe that Tyrone had done this to her.

"Oh my God, what happened to her!!! Destiny shouted in a combination of pure disgust and fear. "Look!!! Destiny I don't have time to explain this shit to you right now!!! I need for you to help me get her to the car!!" He said to his girlfriend as he bent down to help Shawn up.

"Shawn...baby, its Darius. I'm going to take you to the hospital." He said to her as he picked her up in his arms. Darius could not believe Tyrone would do this shit. He felt his blood boiling. If he could have, he would have choked the life right from his friend's body.

They were able to get Shawn to the car and they rushed her to the hospital to get medical attention. When they arrived at the hospital, Patrick, Tyrone's step-father was on call and was immediately paged to the emergency room.

When he rushed to the emergency unit and saw the patient he was instantaneously taken back. He did expect to see his son's ex-girlfriend lying on the table before him. Patrick re-evaluated her chart and was able to stabilize her.

After he was able to attend to her wounds he walked out to the lobby to find out what happened to her. He walked in the lobby and saw Darius, but not Tyrone.

"Hey, Darius!! Why are you here and not Tyrone?!!" He asked as the two men gave each other a pound and embraced. Darius looked at the man who treated him like he was a part of the family and didn't know how to tell him about his son.

"Look, Dr. James let me talk to you in private outside. Destiny, can you please wait for me in here while I talk to him." Destiny looked at her man and did not raise any fuss. She took her seat in the lobby and allowed the men to talk.

Darius and Patrick walked outside over to the doctor's parking area. They got into Patrick's 750I BMW and they began to talk.

"Dr. James, I don't know how to tell you this, but Tyrone is the reason why Shawn is in the hospital." He said. Patrick did not understand what Darius was saying. He heard what he said, but the words were not registering to his brain. Darius told Patrick everything and once they were finished talking they walked their separate ways.

Patrick went back into the hospital and checked on Shawn. He had to hear it from Shawn's mouth. Did his stepson do this to her? He walked up

to her bed and held her hand. He looked at a girl who was beautiful, but you could not tell how beautiful she was because her face was so swollen.

Patrick held her hand and stoked her hair. He had contacted her parents and they were on their way. "Shawn...can you hear me? This is Dr. James...Tyrone's father." He said. Shawn looked at him and smiled. She liked Dr. James and did not hold him or his wife responsible for what their son did to her.

"Honey... how are you feeling?" He asked. She opened her mouth and spoke for the first time since she arrived at the hospital. "I feel a little better. I'm still a little shaken up though." She said as she tried to sit up in the bed.

Dr. James quickly helped her raise her body up enough for her to sit in the bed. When she was comfortable he took a seat next to her bed. The room was silent and he finally found the strength to ask her about Tyrone.

"Shawn... did Tyrone do this do you?!" He asked already knowing the answer in his heart. Shawn looked at Dr. James and she could see the hurt in his eyes. She never thought she would suffer any harm at the hands of Tyrone. If he would have allowed her to speak she would have told him that she had broken up with Davion that day and she wanted to be back with him.

"Mr. James, I love Tyrone and I never meant to hurt him. When I broke up with him, I just needed some space so I could make sure that he was the one for me." She said. Patrick was quiet. He wanted Shawn to remain calm.

"If you don't want to talk about this…you don't have to Shawn. I won't press the issue." He told her. Shawn looked at him and said, "Mr. James, I know you and Mrs. James are good parents to all of your children. I don't blame either one of you for what Tyrone did. I just want him to get some help." As she was talking to him, her parents walked in the room and Patrick knew it was time for him to leave.

After he was done checking on Shawn he walked briskly to his office. He was still trying to wrap his head around what Darius had told him and what Shawn confirmed. He could not believe Tyrone would have done this shit. He was having déjàvu again.

He picked up his office phone and called his attorney. Patrick knew Tyrone was going to need representation. After he got off the phone with the attorney he gathered his things and went home to tell Vasthai what was going on.

Getting Ready for War
Chapter 3

Vasthai walked into her childhood bedroom. She smiled as she remembered the good times she had with her father, grandmother, and her friend Simone.

She walked toward the bed. When she was close enough she bent down and pulled out a shoe box from underneath the bed. Vasthai went to the bedroom door and made sure it was locked. After securely making sure her father could not walk in; she sat on the bed and opened the box.

The contents in the box held invaluable information she needed in her quest to redeem her womanhood from the one person who stole it from her when she was sixteen. Thanks to the Internet and an endless supply of cash, Vasthai was able to research her prey.

She had been collecting information for over a year. Now she was ready to commence destruction on the one person who had given her the most precious gift...but had violated her inner sanctuary in the process.

She took out the pictures looking at them one by one. Then she took out the chess board and placed it on the floor. Vasthai slid to the floor and cut out the faces on the pictures and strategically placed the faces on the board.

She was playing this game for keeps and planned it as if she were a "professor of chess." There was one picture she did not place on the board. She looked at the picture and a tear formed in her eye. Vasthai sighed and placed the picture in her purse.

For many years she had gone on with her life. In her first years of marriage, she had a hard time fully trusting her husband. But as she and Patrick grew as a couple she began to let her guard down. Vasthai slowly realized that all men were not the same and she had grown to love her husband with her complete soul.

Vasthai decided to let the past lie in the past until she received a call from a woman two years prior. She had just come home from church on a Sunday afternoon with her family when the house phone rang. As she reached for the phone she did not look at the Caller ID. Vasthai answered and when she spoke "hello" into the receiver, a woman asked for her by name.

She began to replay the conversation in her mind. *"Vasthai, I know what happened to you when you were sixteen. There is only one question I want to ask you. Do you ever wonder what it would be like to kill your rapist?"The voice said.*

Before she could respond the line went dead. Vasthai was greatly disturbed by the call. She thought she had gotten beyond the pain of her past, but when the woman asked about killing the man who raped her, there was an inner beast awakened. It was on that day Vasthai decided she needed

closure. She would only get that when she killed the man who damaged her.

After placing the contents back in the box, she opened the bedroom door and headed back to her home. Vasthai had a few loose ends to tie up before heading to see her son Tyrone. She was excited about her trip, but she was also going there to let the games begin.

Two weeks later Vasthai was in Atlanta on a flight layover. She was headed to see her son at the FCI Yazoo City Medium Security Prison located in Yazoo City, Mississippi. Her connecting flight was scheduled to take off in fifteen minutes.

She went to the restroom. When she exited the ladies room she heard the intercom calling for all the first-class passengers to board the plane. Vasthai grabbed her ticket and headed for the plane going to Mississippi.

As she was on the plane in her first-class seat she began to think about where she was going. She was going to visit her son in prison. Vasthai knew it was time for him to know the truth. Although, she was exposing herself, she knew Tyrone had to know.

She was deep in thought when the stewardess approached her seat and asked, "May I get you anything to drink or eat?" Vasthai smiled at the young lady and said, "Yes, let me have an Apple Martini and some steamed shrimp." As Vasthai waited for her order, she anxiously anticipated her visit with her son.

Tyrone was outside with the other inmates doing his daily workout. He had no idea how he

was able to stay in the general population being that he was in prison for rape. It was common knowledge that rapists and child molesters were considered the lowest of the low. If it were found out that you were either one of these criminals, you were in a world of shit.

Tyrone was young and green to the world of imprisonment when he entered the penitentiary, but he quickly became acquainted with prison life. He went in as a boy and became a hardened man locked up behind bars. He was unaware he was going to receive a visit. Tyrone went about his daily routine. Little did he know, he was about to hear a story that he was not ready to hear.

Vasthai arrived in Jackson at about nine in the evening and she checked into the Marriott. She got in her room, placed her bags in the middle of the floor, and laid down on the king size bed.

Vasthai looked at the ceiling, closed her eyes, and saw flashes of her life. She smiled as she saw so many good memories going through her mind. Then there was one single tear that rolled down the side of her cheek. That one tear represented the vengeance she internalized and the retribution she had yet to see fulfilled.

"So you think I forgot!!! I never forgot!! Although, I have moved on with my life…I never forgot!! You will reap what you sow!!" She said out loud to herself as she wiped the single tear from her eye. Vasthai needed to get some sleep. She had been travelling the majority of the day and was tired.

She went in the bathroom, turned on the water in the tub, and waited until it was full. Vasthai went to the bar and fixed herself a drink. She soaked in the tub for an hour and once she was done went to bed. She was going to need her strength for her long day.

There is no peace, saith the Lord, for the Wicked...
Isaiah 48:22
Chapter 4

Kennedy was sitting at her desk when the phone rang. She had been waiting for this call for over an hour. Before she answered the phone she walked from her desk and closed her office door. This was a private conversation she needed to take without interruption.

She went into her purse and pulled out the TracPhone. "Hello." She said as she reclined in her plush leather chair. "Yeah, she got the package of information and she arrived in Jackson about an hour ago." The man replied from the other end.

Kennedy smiled because she had prayed that her scheming would encourage Vasthai to come to the city. Although, she had no idea what she had planned, Kennedy hoped whatever it was that it would involve the use of legal services.

"Did you get the package I sent you?" She asked. The man was silent for a minute and said, "Yea, I got it yesterday. So are we squared away?" He asked.

Kennedy was quiet before she answered the question. She needed to be sure she did not need his services anymore.

"Rodney, I will be there to see you this afternoon so we can wrap this up. I will see you in a few hours." She told him as the line went dead.

It was 4:45 in the afternoon. Rodney was sitting at the bar, drinking a Hennessy and Coke; when he saw Kennedy walk through the doors. They had met at this same bar several times before and now it was time for their business relationship to come to an end.

Kennedy saw Rodney and walked over to the bar stool next to him. She sat down and ordered an Amaretto Sour. Once she got her drink she headed over to a secluded booth in the corner of the bar.

Rodney waited until she was seated in the booth before walking over to join her. There was a momentary silence between them as they sipped on their drinks.

"So what's up? I did my part of the deal. Now it is time for you to fulfill your end of the bargain." Rodney said as he looked at the woman sitting in front of him.

Kennedy studied him and looked into his eyes. His eyes showed the window of his soul. What she saw, was a man who was from the old school, a man of principles, a man whose words were his bond.

Kennedy thought to herself what would make him risk his license to practice psychiatric medicine and provide her with the information she

requested. It was probably the $300,000 dollars in cash she was paying him. That was a big incentive.

Kennedy was a lawyer and knew the law. She knew the information she obtained from Rodney was gotten illegally. She did not want any paper trail connecting them; so she decided to pay him in cash.

Kennedy did her research on her target by investigating Rodney's confidential employee file. That's how she discovered that HE was one of Rodney's patients. With the information in her possession, she made Dr. Jenkins a proposition.

"Let me ask you a question. What made you break your oath of doctor /patient confidentiality and work with me?" She asked as she sipped on the last of her drink and summoned the waitress to place another order.

Rodney also drowned the last of his drink and ordered another Hennessy and Coke. He was quiet as he pondered the question that was posed to him.

"Let me tell you something Kennedy. I was raised in the heart of the ghetto in Detroit and I have come across some of the hardest criminals. Most of them were a product of their environment; just trying to survive the ghetto. When I started to the practice medicine I came into contact with many patients who were mentally deranged. But when you treat a person who has the mental capacity to brutally attack a woman... like she was a maimed beast... and take her pussy... that is one man who needs to be put out of his misery. It's like my

mother always told me *"There is no peace, saith the Lord, for the Wicked..."*

Let me tell you a story
Chapter 5

It was 9:30 in the morning when Vasthai ordered room service to her hotel room. She was up early but she was not in a hurry to drive the hour to see Tyrone.

She had made prior arrangements with the proper people and was granted unlimited visiting time with her son, so she was not in any rush. She sat in the bed and ate her big country breakfast. Vasthai was getting her mind right for the day.

" Tyrone James, you have a visitor!!" The CO shouted as the cell opened. Tyrone did not say a word. He turned around and let the CO handcuff him. They walked down the prison corridor passing the other prisoners in their cells.

Tyrone looked at the CO and said, "Yo... who is here to see me?" The CO never answered his question. He just led him to an empty waiting room. The CO took the handcuffs off of him and he stepped back into the corner.

The room was large, but dimly lit. Tyrone sat in his chair, looked around, and wondered what the fuck was going on. He stood up from his chair and when he did; he saw a woman walk in the room. At first, he could not make out who the

woman was. It was apparent who she was once she got closer.

Tyrone ran to his mother and hugged her for dear life. He was so excited to see her. "What are you doing here?!"He asked her as they both sat down at the provided table.

Vasthai looked at her son. She could tell he was not the same as he was before he got locked up. She just wanted to look at her handsome son. It had been so long since she saw him in person.

"Do I have to have a reason to see my son?!! I got your letter and wanted to see you." She said as she walked over to the correctional officer and whispered something in his ear. The CO smiled and walked out the room leaving Vasthai and Tyrone alone.

Vasthai walked back to the table and sat in front of her son. She was happy to see him. Vasthai went into her purse, pulled out a box of Newports, and handed Tyrone one. They both lit up and inhaled the smoke through their nostrils.

Tyrone looked into his mother's eyes and knew there was something on her mind. "Mom, I know you are here to see me, but I can tell there is something wrong. What's the deal?" He said. It was true she was there for a purpose but, Vasthai wanted to enjoy her cigarette before she got down to the real reason why she came.

"Well, I see you know me well!!! Since you want me to cut the bullshit and get right down to real… lets begin then."Vasthai responded as she put out the Newport in the ashtray.

"Tyrone, you are my oldest son. I have protected you and made sure you had a good life. I love all of my children unconditionally. You have always been my heart. When I got your letter... your father told me it was time for you to know everything." She said.

Tyrone looked at his mother with a confused look on his face. He had no idea where she was going with the conversation. He wanted to ask questions, but his instincts told him; if he listened all of his questions would be answered.

Tyrone grabbed another Newport and began to smoke it. He blew the smoke in his mother's face and said, "I'm listening." Vasthai sat back in her chair and responded, "Let me tell you a story." With that said, she was about to give Tyrone the unadulterated truth.

The Birthday Girl
September 19, 1986
Chapter 6

It was three o'clock and fifteen minutes before school was done for the day. Vasthai was excited because she had just turned sixteen. "Thai what is your father getting you for your birthday"? Simone asked her friend, already knowing about the surprise party her father was giving her on Saturday at the spot.

"All I know is I'm suppose to be getting the new Michael Jordan's. I already got my hair done and a new outfit earlier this week. James brought me roses, a stuffed teddy bear, and gave me money the other day at school. Other than that, I don't know." She said.

Vasthai and Simone had been friends since elementary school. They were the two flyest girls in their school. Vasthai was the only child, while Lisa was the eldest of three siblings with a father who was a revered hustler.

They became friends in the third grade when Larry, Simone's father, brought his Lincoln Towncar into Vasthai's fathers' auto mechanic shop. Since then, Larry and Russell had been friends and their daughters also became the best of friends.

The bell rang signaling that school was done for the day. Vasthai and Simone gathered their things and headed out the doors of Ely High. They were greeted by James as soon as they walked out the door into the parking lot.

"Hey, Boo what's up?!!" Vasthai said to James her boyfriend of almost a year. He pulled her in his arms and smacked her ass. "Nothing!! I'm waiting to tap that fat ass of yours!" He said back. Vasthai rolled her eyes at James.

She liked James, but she wasn't feeling him like that. Since Vasthai was young, her father always talked to her about "game" and how dudes were going to try and "run game" on her. Vasthai was taught well and she always had her guard up.

"Hmmm... I sense you are use to these gutter sluts who you been fucking!! But nigga you will never get the chance to put your dick in this tight warm pussy!! Let alone put your facial hair it!! So if you ever disrespect me again I will cut that little dick of yours off and feed it to the alligators in the swamps!!!" Vasthai yelled at him as she and Simone turned to walk away.

"Dammmmmn!!! She told you nigga!!" His boys shouted through their laughs. "Vasthai!! Where are you going??"James shouted as he ran behind her. He grabbed her and turned her around to face him. It was true James wanted to add Vasthai to his fuck list. He thought it would have happened by now but, she was proving to be harder than the rest of the broads he usually got. James had to put in extra work, but he was determined to be the first to fuck that virgin pussy.

"Look, I'm sorry. I was just playing with you." He said. Vasthai was not convinced. She knew he was hungry to fuck her. There were a few times she was even considering letting him be her first, but lately she was trying to find a way to get rid of his ass.

"Whatever, James!! I don't play like that!! As a matter of fact, this relationship is not working for me." She responded back. Simone and James both looked at Vasthai. They both figured where the conversation was heading and it did not look good for James.

James kept his composure. He smiled and grabbed her hand. "What are you saying Thai?" He said as their eyes met. "Like I said, this is not working for me. So from this point on … it's over!!" Vasthai took her hand back and grabbed Simone by the arm. The two of them walked off heading toward Vasthai's house.

James was stood there dumbfounded. He was humiliated by a high and uppity bitch. He had no intentions of letting her get away with that shit. At that moment he knew exactly what he was going to do to her. When he did…he was going to leave his mark.

****

Vasthai looked across the table at her son. Tyrone had been listening to his mother talk for the last two hours. He could tell she was talking about something was very painful for her.

He looked around to see if the CO was back to take him to his cell. Tyrone was surprised to see they were still alone in the room. He did not ask

how he was able to have such a long visitation with his mother. Something told him that his mother had made some back room deals in order for him to hear this story face to face.

A Sheep Among A Wolf
Chapter 7

Vasthai looked at her Blackberry and saw she was receiving a phone call. She looked at the number and quickly pressed the ignore button. She become agitated and it showed by her facial expression.

Tyrone looked at her and said, "Who was that on the phone? I see that you are upset." Vasthai looked at her son. She loved him, but he could be extremely nosy and she did not need him in her business.

"You don't need to worry about who is calling my phone!!! Let me handle my business and you handle yours." She told him.

He was taken back by her response. They were always close. Tyrone could not understand why she was tripping about what he asked her. "My bad!! I was hoping it was daddy calling. I really want to talk to my sister and brother." He said to her.

Vasthai felt bad for going off but she was not there for idle chit-chat. She was there to tell her story. "Look...baby, I want to finish talking to you and I don't want any interruptions. I hope you can understand this." She stated, trying to break the awkwardness between them.

It was silent in the room. Vasthai cleared her throat and continued the story. "It was the Friday before my surprise party and your Paw-Paw had taken me to get my license. I excited and passed the exam on my first try." She paused to make sure he was listening. When Vasthai was sure she had his undivided attention, she continued.

"Simone had come over to the house later that day and we gossiped in my room. Simone had informed me that James started a rumor about me around school." Vasthai said.

"Girl....you know James is going around saying that he fucked you!!" Simone told her friend. Vasthai was not shocked by what he was saying, but what he forgot to say was that he was the one eating her pussy and sticking his tongue in the crack of her ass. It was true, Vasthai was a freak, but she was a freak who had not had sex yet.

"The nigga is just mad because he wanted to fuck me and he didn't!! I don't pay attention to bitch ass niggas!!! I'm glad I cut him loose!!" Vasthai said as she passed the joint back to Simone.

Vasthai and Simone had the house to themselves because their dads had gone out. When they got together they spent the whole night out partying and fucking. The two of them smoked the joint, lit up another one, and ended up falling asleep on the bed.

Vasthai looked at her watch and read the time. It was one in the morning. She was tired and she needed to head back. "Look, I'm tired, I'm going to leave for tonight, but tomorrow I will be

back to finish this conversation." Like clock work, the CO appeared to take Tyrone back to his cell.

"Excuse me!!" The CO said to Vasthai. She turned and looked at him. "You look familiar. Where have I seen you before?" He asked. She looked at him and smiled, but never responded to his question.

Vasthai kissed her son and stood in front of the CO and Tyrone. She looked at the CO with the eyes of Satan and said, "Don't worry honey... you will know me!!!" With those words she walked to exit the room.

The CO and Tyrone were both shocked. Her statement had come from left field. Tyrone was led back to his cell for the night.

Correctional Officer Williams was ending his shift and was about to head home. He was getting his things ready but he kept hearing the words of the woman in his head who visited Tyrone.

IT was not the words she said but how she said them... as if she was threatening him. "The bitch must be crazy!!" He said. Williams opened his locker to get his duffle bag. When he opened the duffle bag he saw a wrapped box with a black bow around it.

"What the fuck is this!!" He shouted. Williams picked the box up and noticed it was light in weight. He looked around the room to see if anyone was watching. Williams realized he was alone and opened the box. He looked inside the box and his eyes got wide. He placed his hand over his mouth to prevent himself from gagging.

Williams took his hand away from his mouth and understood why he felt the urge to vomit. The box contained a pair of dirty, fishy, and pissy smelling pair of women underwear. "Who the fuck put this shit in my bag!!!?? Who the fuck is playing games!!" He wondered.

He walked to where the cleaning supplies were. He grabbed a pair of rubber gloves and put them on his hands. Williams was still visibly upset when he stormed over to his bag and snatched the underwear up.

He proceeded to place them in a plastic bag when he saw a note pinned to the crouch. He looked at the note and read the words… "*I NEVER FORGOT.*"

Williams was silent as the foul things he had done in the past cluttered his thoughts. He thought he was not the same man he once was; and he tried everyday to redeem his wrongs. He didn't know, the more he tried to run from his past, the closer he was running to his demise.

Williams composed himself enough to get his things and head out the door. He took the plastic bag with the underwear in it and threw them in the dumpster on the way to his car. When he got to the parking lot he did not see his car in the spot where he parked it at the beginning of his shift. Williams pushed the button on his keychain and the chirping from the alarm caught his attention.

He walked to his car and began to smell the overwhelming scent of shit. Williams reached his car and dropped his bag to the ground. The smell was coming from his car. His car was covered in a

combination of dog, cow, cat, and human feces. Every part of his car was covered in it except for the driver side door handle.

"Who is fucking stalking me?!!! Bitch whoever you are... I will cut that rotten fish hole of a pussy from your body!!!" He yelled as he continued to inspect his car. As he was examining the car, Chris one of the other guards, was also walking to his car to head home. As Chris got closer to his car, he also smelled the overpowering stench of shit.

"Yo!! Williams do you smell that?!!" Chris said as he walked to his SUV that was parked four cars down from Williams. Chris did not get a response from Williams and he quickly saw why. He walked up to where Williams was standing and saw the condition of his car.

"Man...what the hell happened here?" Chris asked as he looked at his co-worker. Williams looked at his car and said, "Shit!! I done pissed off some bitch, cause this is definitely the work of a crazy ass bitch!! I just hope it's not Monica doing this to me. I stopped fucking her and now she wants to break up my happy home with my wife."

Chris looked at the car and shook his head. He had warned him before about fucking those busted broads. All he knew was, Williams had a good woman at home, and he was going to lose her if he could not control his dick. "Look man... you make sure you take this piece of shit to the carwash before you get home!!" Chris said, laughing out loud.

Williams looked at Chris and laughed back saying, "Nigga you think this shit is funny!! Well its not!! You can suck my dick!!" The two men went their separate ways to their cars and drove off.

Williams was not even out the parking lot when he saw the words: *I'M GOING TO SHIT ON YOU* carved in his dashboard. By now he was too done. It was confirmed. He was on someone's shit list!!! Williams sped off, hauling ass to the nearest drive- thru carwash.

When he pulled into the driveway of his house he noticed the door was slightly cracked. Williams was immediately alarmed and grabbed his gun. When he walked in the door he saw that everything was intact inside.

He quickly walked through the house checking on his daughter and then his wife. When he saw they were alright he went to close and lock the front door. Williams sat down on the couch and took off his work shoes.

He was getting comfortable so he could watch Sports Center before getting in the bed. Williams went in the kitchen to pour himself a glass of soda and to look through the mail.

Williams was headed back to the couch when he saw there was an unopened FedEx box sitting on the kitchen table. He finished his drink and walked to the table. The box was addressed to him. Williams looked at the box for the sender's information, but it was left blank.

He knew the box had to be from his stalker. Williams was now paranoid because he had never

let any of his women know where he lived. Now one of them knew where he laid his head!

"I have to find out who this broad is before she blows me up to my wife!!" He said as he ripped open the box. He looked inside the box and his stomach turned. Williams emptied all of his stomach's contents from the day. He was more sickened than upset.

"OH my God!!! That is the nastiest shit I have ever seen!!" He said as he cleaned up his vomit from the kitchen floor. What he saw was mind boggling. Whoever Williams was dealing with was a sick individual. The box contained a bloody tampon with a taped note hanging from the string saying, "I'M GOING TO FUCK YOU...UNTIL YOU BLEED."

After he cleaned up his mess, gargled his mouth with mouthwash; Williams walked in his bedroom to get in bed with his wife Layce.

"Layce... baby wake up." He said to his wife as he climbed on top of her. As she opened her eyes Williams was admiring her beauty. She was beautiful standing at 5'6, 130 pounds with the complexion of rich coca and hazel green eyes. Layce was a dime who was a rider for her husband.

"What's wrong baby?" She asked as she kissed him on his neck. She had been married to Williams for two years but she was his woman for sixteen years before they got married.

Williams never answered her question because he was to busy with his head buried in her pussy. He was sucking on her clit as he stroked his eight inches of manhood with his right hand. The

two of them were so engrossed in their pleasure that they never noticed they had a peeping tom looking at them from the outside.

"Hmmm…Williams I want you inside of me." Layce moaned in her moment of passion. Just when she was about to explode in his mouth, he raised his body from between her open her legs, and plunged into her. They tussled in the sheets for the remainder of night's darkness. When Layce was finally asleep…Williams got up from the bed and walked out the house to smoke a cigarette.

When he opened the front door he saw a picture on the porch. He bent down to retrieve the picture and was looking at him and Layce in the act of fucking. Williams examined the picture further and realized the picture was of them having sex earlier that night.

"What the fuck!!!" Williams looked around to see if there was anyone watching him or the house. He was so nervous he smoked his cigarette too quickly. Williams knew whoever his stalking was; that they were out to get him.

From that moment on he was vulnerable. He was going to be on guard until he could figure out what the hell was going on. He was not willing to lose his family and he was willing to fight to the death to keep it that way!

If You Come With Honey... You Will Always Catch the Bee...

Chapter 8

Vasthai was in her hotel room when she received a call from her husband. She had not spoken to him since the day before. Vasthai put down her food to answer her Blackberry. "Hello". She said.

"Hey Baby! I was calling to see how it is going with Tyrone." He asked her as he sat in his office at their home. Vasthai looked at the white wall as she thought about his question. "Well it's going as well as expected. I will be going back to see him to finish our conversation a little later today." She said.

"Do you need me to come down there for moral support?" Patrick asked as he looked at the family picture of them on his mahogany desk.

Vasthai loved her husband very much but she had no intentions of having him come there. She had other plans that were already set in motion. She did not need anyone else she loved involved in her treachery.

Vasthai learned a long time ago from her father …if you were going to do dirt… you do your dirt by your lonesome.

"No Patrick, it is no need for you to come here. Besides, I will be home soon as I'm finished here. How are my babies, Kamron and Tyson?" She asked trying to change the topic.

"They are fine. They are upset that you did not take them with you. They wanted to see their brother." He replied. Before his wife could respond to his statement Patrick interrupted by saying he had to go because the hospital was paging him. They hung up the phone and Vasthai finished her food.

Back at Williams' House

Layce was cleaning the house before she went to pick up her child from school. As she was cleaning her mind went back to the night of love making she had with her husband.

They had a very active sex life and she was always satisfied with his performance. But last night she felt like his body was there with her but his mind was a million miles away. She could not put her finger on it, but, something was not quite right.

As she thought about the night before she became startled by the ringing of the doorbell. Layce went to the door and peered out the glass foyer window. When she looked out Layce saw a woman standing at the front door.

She opened the door and said, "Yes, may I help you?" Layce said as she sized up the woman. The woman was polite and didn't get an attitude. The woman smiled showing perfectly even white teeth.

"I did not mean to frighten you, but I am a first time home buyer. I was looking for houses to

buy when I saw the for sale sign in your yard." The woman said hoping the suspecting lady would let her inside the house.

Layce became friendlier. They had been trying to sell their house because they were building a bigger house in Jackson and there was no way they could pay two mortgages. "I'm sorry, I was rude to you!! Please come in! My name is Layce and you are?!" She asked the strange woman.

The woman looked around the cozy home and said. "My name is Monica Davis." She told her as she took a seat on the couch. Layce went to the kitchen and poured them a cup of tea and they talked for about an hour.

Monica gave Layce her business card. She asked her to call when it was convenient for Layce to give her a tour of the house. Monica walked to her car and drove off. Layce closed the front door placing the business card on the living room table.

Unbeknown to Layce, she had just let a woman into her home who was hell bent on making her husband pay for his past indiscretions, indiscretions she had no knowledge about.

Layce was about to pull out of the driveway when she saw Williams pull into the driveway from the gym. "Hey baby!" She said to her husband as she walked to his car.

"Where you headed to?" He asked her as he grabbed his gym bag from the car. Layce got in her car and let the window down before she answered. "I'm headed to the school to pick up your daughter then we are going to the mall so I can buy her some shoes." She told him

"Wait let me give you some money so you can buy yourself something." He told her as he went into his wallet and pulled out five one hundred dollar bills. Layce smiled as she eagerly took the money and pulled off.

Williams walked into the house and put down his things. He turned on the television and placed his feet on the table. He turned to Sports Center and watched the latest sports news.

He decided to get up to fix something to drink when he took his foot down from the table and noticed that a card fell to the ground. The card landed in front of his foot. Williams picked the card up and almost had a heart attack when he read the name on the card.

He could not believe it!! Was it true that his mistress had stopped by to pay his wife a visit!!? What did she tell Layce? He was livid and he needed to handle that bitch right then. But if he had looked closer at the card he would have noticed that the number on the card did not belong to Monica.

Williams grabbed his car keys and stormed out the house. As he rode down the street he passed the woman who was known to his wife as Monica Davis but known to him as Vasthai. As his car sped by she knew exactly where he was going. He was headed to pay the real Monica a visit.

The Story Continues
Chapter 9

Tyrone was in his cell thinking about his visit with his mother. He was thinking about the story she started to tell him and right when she was about to reveal something important she stopped. He could feel that something was not right.

Tyrone was preparing his mind for the worst and praying for the best. He was just about to put his hand on his dick and masturbate while looking at a picture of Shawn when the CO came and told him he had a visitor.

He looked at him with a look of annoyance because he was about to bust a nut but he kept his comments to himself. Tyrone turned around so he could be handcuffed.

He was led to the same room he had been in the night before. Tyrone waited for his visitor, his mother. Five minutes later, Vasthai walked in wearing a pair of True Religion boot cut jeans with a True Religion tank top. On her feet she sported a pair of black Jimmy Choo high heels. She looked good with her size eight frame rocking a cute, but, expensive outfit.

She and Tyrone greeted each other, and like the previous day, they were left alone in the room as the CO made his exit. "How are you doing baby?" She asked Tyrone as they both prepared to smoke.

Tyrone took the smoke and said, "I'm fine mom, how about you?" He asked. Vasthai laughed to herself. Tyrone looked as he did when he was younger and trying to get information out of her. "I'm fine baby!!! I am just glad that I am able to see you." She replied.

He looked at his mother and smiled. Tyrone was happy to see her, too, but he was also eager to hear the rest of her story. "So, Mom you were telling me something last night and..." Before he could finish his statement Vasthai held up her hand to stop him. She looked at him and smiled.

"Well let me not keep you waiting!!!" She said while leaning toward him. Vasthai cleared her throat and started her story where she left off. "As I was telling you yesterday. Simone and I had fallen asleep on my bed and the next day was Saturday. The day was going fine. I had no idea my daddy was throwing me a surprise party that night. Simone and I had been out all day getting our hair, nails, toes, and shopping done." Vasthai looked at Tyrone and she saw he was holding his breath.

The room was bathed in silence as each of them enjoyed the smoke from their cigarettes. Tyrone looked around the room and once again, he realized they were alone. In the back of his mind he knew something was up with that, but, he kept his thoughts private.

Vasthai looked into her son's eyes and said, "The night of my surprise party was the night I lost my innocence and became a woman who was immune to pain." Tyrone heard his mother's words, but he is confused as to what she meant.

"So what are you saying!?" He asked her. Vasthai swallowed hard and said, "After we came back from our outing my father blind folded me. He told me he had something for me. Daddy, Simone, Simone's father and I got into the car and rode out. I was too excited because I thought was getting a car. When we stepped out of the car and into the skating rink my blind fold was lifted and everyone shouted surprise!"

Vasthai got up from her seat and walked over to the wall and stood against it. She closed her eyes and replayed that night in her mind. As her eyes were closed she opened her mouth, "Let me just get to the point Tyrone! I was at the party laughing and having a good time until James came into the rink. We locked eyes but did not speak. He and I eyed each other as we passed by each other." She stated.

Tyrone was listening to each word that was coming from her mouth. He not only wanted to know but he had to know. "Why didn't you approach him about coming to the party?" He asked. Vasthai thought about his question but she had no answer.

"I don't know why I didn't approach him. What I do know is, he came up to me and we walked over to a spot away from everyone else. We sat down in one of the empty booths. We never spoke because I was on the verge of busting a nut while he played in my pussy." Vasthai walked back over to her seat and sat down.

"I had raised my skirt higher so he could have better access to me. I was enjoying his touch

so much that I did not feel myself falling into a subdued unconsciousness. What I remember next was James and I walking out of the skating rink and into his car. When I opened my eyes again I was in a strange place. All I saw were faces of different men." Vasthai looked into her son's eyes for his reaction, but what she saw was his poker face.

Tyrone did not say a word. His mind was going in all directions but he could not articulate his thoughts. Instead, he sat patiently waiting for his mother to say what happened next. "When I tried to get up I couldn't because I was tied to a chair. I was afraid and I began to call out for my dad and Simone. When I yelled out their names I immediately felt a blow to my face. When I looked up I saw James standing over me. He looked at me and said, "So you thought you were going to get away with cutting me off!!! Bitch I tell you when it's over!!! I'm about to show you how to be a woman and not some silly ass little girl!!" He told me as he slapped me continuously across my face.

"As he hit me I began praying to God for him to stop. When James did stop he grabbed my clothes and tore them from my body. He was looking at my titties when he said, "Don't worry you are, going to enjoy this!!"

"I was so scared. I did not know what to do or expect. I closed my eyes and my mind went to a place that was peaceful. James untied me from the chair, threw me to the concrete ground, and told me to get on my knees. I did as I was told. When I was on my knees I could feel someone else's hands touching my body. The man's hands were rough on

my skin. I tried to look at his face and I was punched and kicked until I could do nothing but curl up in the fetal position."

"I was shocked out of my coma-like condition when I felt the worst pain shooting through my body. I discovered that I was being held on my knees again as James was pumping his dick inside of me and the other man was fucking me in my ass! I cried and screamed for them to stop, but they continued to assault my body."

"When the stranger was done he ejaculated in my ass and left me there with James. I laid there on the ground for what seemed like hours as he fucked me in every which way he could think of, and when he was done he left me there...alone, cold, and raped."

Tyrone was in shock. He could not believe what he was hearing!! His mother just told him she was raped! He did not know how to feel. At that moment he was numb. Tyrone grabbed his mother's hand trying to console her.

Vasthai wiped the tears that were falling from her eyes. "I was able to pull myself to the light that was coming from the door. I was so weak that I passed out as soon as I reached the door. When I woke up I was in the hospital."

Vasthai let go of Tyrone's hand and looked at him. She could see that he was torn and confused. "Tyrone...the night I was raped... I conceived you!!! You were the best thing that came out of that situation. When I married Patrick he loved you as if you were his own and he never let anyone tell him differently." That was the first time Vasthai

admitted to Tyrone that Patrick was not his biological father.

Patrick was her doctor when she was in the hospital and he vowed to make her his wife. They dated as Vasthai recovered. After Tyrone was born he played father to her son. With his help, the support of her father, and Simone; Vasthai was able to slowly recover from her wounds. When she turned eighteen after graduating from high school they were married. Although, Vasthai was able to recover from her physical damage, she would never get over the mental torture.

Tyrone was enraged. He had just learned that the man who loved and raised him was not his father. To add insult to his injury he just heard he was a rapist just like his biological father.

"What!!! You mean to tell me that all of these years you led me to believe that my father was my father but he isn't!!! Now I have a defect in my genes because I have committed the same fucking crime as my father!!" He shouted out to his mother.

Vasthai knew Tyrone was hurt, but, he needed to know the truth. "Tyrone, sit down!!" She told him. He looked at her as if they were enemies but did as he was told. "Look, I know you are hurt, but, your father is still your father. I just wanted to tell you about James, because I want you to understand where you got your behavior from. If there is someone you need to be mad with, then you take your frustrations out on me... not your father... ever!!!" She told him.

Tyrone took his mother's words to heart. She was right... his father was not the issue. The

nigga whose nut sack he came from was. He made up in his mind that if his mother ever told him more information about his biological father again… that he would take mental notes. Now he wanted to meet him so he could kill him.

"Are you going to tell me who he is?" Tyrone asked her. Vasthai looked at her son and said, "No, not right now. I think you need some time for this to digest. When the time is right… you will know exactly who he is. When you find out who he is, you do what you have to do!!" She told Tyrone with a sexy smirk spreading across her lips.

Black Boot Stomp
The Door Down
Chapter 10

Monica was just getting out of the shower when she heard a loud beating sound at her front door. The volume of the banging scared the shit out of her. Before she could grab her robe and hurry to the door… she was bombarded with a forceful blow to her face by James.

She almost hit her head on her bathroom sink when she fell to the floor. Monica had no idea what just happened to her, but, when she looked up she saw James hovering over her. What she saw in his eyes was a look of rage. Before she could ask what was going on he hit her again.

"What the fuck!!! You come to my house and talk to my wife!! What the fuck do you think this shit is!! When I told you that it was over, I meant that shit!!" James shouted at her as he grabbed her by her neck.

Monica had no idea what he was talking about. They had broken up three weeks ago. Yes, she was upset that James dumped her, but she quickly picked up her feelings and was trying to move on with her life.

"What are you talking about James?! This is the first time I have seen you in almost a month!!"

She said to him as she tried to catch her breath as he gripped his hand around her neck.

James was so enraged that he ignored her words and continued to hit her. Monica tried to fight him back, but her blows did not deter him. With his hand still around her neck James forced her mouth open. With his free hand he unzipped his pants and pulled out his dick.

James was always aroused when he was in complete control over women. The power that he held over them made his dick rock hard. He ignored Monica's pleas for him to stop and plunged his dick into her mouth.

With his hand still on her neck he forced her face to suck his dick. "Suck this shit bitch!! Lick my nuts and take this dick!!" He told her as he felt his orgasm coming to a head. James removed his dick from her mouth, plunged it inside her pussy, and deposited his seed into her vaginal opening.

When James was done he took the towel from around her body and wiped away his sperm.
He turned, looked at her, and said, "Monica, don't make me have to come back here again!!!! If you continue to try and break up my family I will cut your nipples off and let you die slow!!!" He released her neck, walked out the bathroom, and back to his car.

Monica was hysterical!! She had just been violated by the man she loved and the attack was for no reason whatsoever. She picked herself up from the floor; went to the front door, and locked it back. Monica walked back into her bathroom and started

the shower again. Once the water was hot enough she got in.

She was unable to wash her body of all of the filth she felt. Monica was devastated by what had just taken place. She tried to put the images of James attacking her out of her mind but she couldn't.

Monica slid down the wall of the shower and sat in the tub. She clinched her knees to her chest and cried. She cried until her tears could no longer come from her eyes.

James went to wok at the prison as if nothing happened. He clocked in and started his shift. In his mind, he just resolved a problem before the problem got out of hand.

What he didn't realize was, his sins were adding up daily, and he would have to take responsibility for his actions. He was going to face his purgatory; his own personal hell on earth.

Uniting for a Common Cause
Chapter 11

Monica was at her job trying to pick up the pieces of her life. She took a week of personal leave from her job, hoping to get past her attack. The more she tried to forget, the more humiliated she felt. She still had no idea why James Williams had attacked her.

It had been a month since her ordeal and she was maintaining her sanity. Monica had just gotten off a conference call with one of her clients. Monica was a District Attorney. Before she became the DA, she was one of the best defense attorneys in the state.

She met James when she went to the prison to confer with one of her clients. The chemistry between them was apparent and shortly after their first meeting James was in her bed.

Monica was attracted to his physical appearance. James was a medium brown complexioned man, who stood 6'2, with a muscular physique. His eyes were a deep brown and his lips said, "Put your pussy on my tongue." Monica never took into account about his home life. All she wanted was James.

As time progressed and their relationship grew, Monica found herself falling in love with

him. When he told her it was over, she was heartbroken.

"Excuse me...Ms. Davis." Monica's receptionist said interrupting her thoughts. "What's up Shannon?" She asked her.

"There is a woman here to see you. She said that it is important that she speaks with you, but she won't give me her name." She stated while she looked at her boss for direction on how to handle the situation.

Monica got up from her chair and walked out of her office door. When she walked into the waiting area a woman stood and extended her hand.

"Ms. Davis, my name is Vasthai James. I am here to speak with you about a mutual problem that we both have. I think we can help each other in solving our issue." Vasthai said as she released Monica's hand.

Monica was confused. This was a woman whom she never met before and here she was telling her that they had a problem...what the hell!!!

"I'm sorry, Ms. James. I don't seem to understand." Monica responded waiting for clarification.

"Ms. Davis, if we could step into your office for more privacy, I will be more than happy to explain." Vasthai told her, as she stepped closer to her office door.

For some reason Monica felt as if the woman standing before her was there for a specific reason that concerned her. She was intrigued by what she had to say. The two women did not say

another word. They walked into Monica's office and closed the door behind them.

Once in the office Monica asked Vasthai to have a seat and offered her something to drink. When they were settled Vasthai got down to business. "Ms. Davis, I know that you do not know me. However, you and I both have one person in common. You see, I am quite aware of what he did to you." She said, as she looked Monica dead in the eyes.

Monica had not told a soul about how James attacked her, and she knew he damn sure was not about to tell on himself. So what did she know about her? "I'm sorry, Ms. Jackson. I don't understand where you are coming from?" Monica said to Vasthai as she tried to deflect attention away from her.

Vasthai looked at the woman who was sitting across from her and smiled. "Look!!! I am not here to bring up any bad memories for you, but honey, I know what James did to you!" She stated. When Vasthai mentioned James' name Monica's mouth flew open. She never said his name.

"May I call you Vasthai?" Monica asked her. She nodded her head in approval and she proceeded. "Vasthai, I don't know how you know what you think you know, but I have no issue with Mr. Williams. If you are here to convince me that I have a problem with him; I am going to have to ask you to leave." Monica told her as she stood up from her seat expecting her guest to leave.

Vasthai reached into her purse and produced a picture of Monica in her house on the day that she

was attacked. She threw the picture down on the desk. Monica saw the picture and tears began filling her eyes. How could she know something so private about her? She was speechless and could not bring herself to speak.

Vasthai handed her a Kleenex for her tears. "Monica, I'm not here to embarrass you or to make you feel ashamed. This was not your fault! If you trust me... you and I can both get this grimy nigga!!" Vasthai told her.

Monica was confused. She wondered how she knew about the rape and she wondered why she wanted to get James so badly?

"Vasthai, I have no idea how you know about this incident, but I want no part in what you are plotting. Why should I even trust you?" She asked.

When Monica asked that question, Vasthai knew she had her. "Monica, I'm going to keep it 100 with you. I know you don't know me. For all you know, I am here to blackmail you or something. Let's get this straight off the rip. My husband and I are quite well off and I don't need a motherfucking thing from you. Additionally, I know you want that punk ass, bitch nigga to pay for violating you." She said to her.

Monica heard what Vasthai was saying. Yes, she did want him to pay, but what did Vasthai have in mind for him. Monica had so many thoughts roaming through her mind. As she was about to speak; Vasthai stopped her.

"I understand that this is a lot to take in. If you decide to work with me, call me on this phone;

at this number." Vasthai placed a burner cell phone and business card on the desk.

She got up to leave when Monica said, "What's in this for you?" She stopped in her tracks and turned around to face her. "Monica, I see that you are an attorney, and as an attorney you have to do research on your cases. Think of me as your special project. But let me; let you in on a little secret. James Williams is and always will be a fucking rapist!!! Just so you know...you are not the only one he has placed his dick in forcefully." Vasthai reached inside of her Fendi purse and pulled out another picture.

Monica looked at the picture and could not believe what she was seeing! The picture was of James fucking what looked to be a young girl under the age of sixteen. The girl was fully developed, but her face showed that she was just a baby. It was then that Monica knew she was going to call her newfound ally.

Vasthai saw the look on her face and knew exactly what she was thinking. "I will be expecting your call tonight. We will meet so I can tell you exactly what I want you to do." She said what she needed to say and walked out of Monica's office.

Vasthai walked to her car smiling. She could not help but laugh on the inside. Her plan was coming together beautifully. She could not wait to see the fruits of her labor materialized.

"Damn!!! It's amazing what PhotoShop can do to a picture!!!" She said out loud to herself. The picture she gave to Monica of James and the little

girl was actually a picture of James and Layce fucking.

The picture of her was an old picture stolen from her house. But when Vasthai got done editing the photos, Layce looked like a sweet and tender twelve year old girl and Monica looked as if she were attacked.

"This nigga has no idea what I have in store for his sorry ass!!" She said as she cranked up her rental car and drove off.

Revenge So Sweet...My Pussy is Dripping in my Juices

Chapter 12

Monica waited for Vasthai to arrive at Starbucks. When she left her office earlier that day she was filled with horror. She kept thinking; how could she be so blind to this man's ways? As she was trying to rationalize her relationship with James, Vasthai walked up and sat down.

"Good Evening." She said greeting Monica with a smile.

"I'm feeling better, but, I want to know what you have planned for James." Monica replied.

Vasthai liked Monica. She could tell that she was a woman about her business and not about the bullshit. She was a woman after her own heart.

Vasthai placed a laptop on top of the table. She booted the machine up and opened the Microsoft Word program. "I don't like talking about things that can incriminate me in public. I typed your directions down in this document." She stated as she turned the laptop facing Monica.

Monica read the document and smiled. She was unsure as to what Vasthai's full plan was, but, she was willing to do her part in destroying her ex-

lover. When she was done reading the message Monica turned the laptop back around to Vasthai.

"No, I want you to keep this laptop. This computer has been encrypted so no one can hack it and everything on there cannot be traced. This means, I am going to email the time and date for this *event,* so don't worry. Nothing will be traced back to either one of us. When everything is over you can burn it." Vasthai told her.

As Monica was shutting the laptop down, Vasthai got up from the table. She reached into her purse and placed on the table an envelope of money, another cell phone burner, and another business card with a different phone number on it.

"What's all of this?" Monica asked as she looked at the items that were placed in front of her. Vasthai sat back down in her seat and whispered, "The envelope should be enough to cover your fees. The cell is for me to call you. The card is the number from which I will call you from. Don't use either one of the burners for personal use. The phones are only to be used for me to call you." Vasthai said as answered her question in full detail. Monica and Vasthai left Starbucks, each one of them envisioning James' world crashing down.

Vasthai went back to her hotel room and called her husband and children. She needed to hear their voices. After her call home she placed another call to her expected company.

She knew she could not return home until she finished what she started out to do. After, she was off the phone; Vasthai found herself looking in the full length mirror.

She was beautiful. She was a pecan brown, 5'5, 145 pounds, with dark brown slanted eyes. When she was younger, her father always told her about her Japanese mother. She never asked the reason why her mother was not in *their* life.

Vasthai found herself examining her body. She began to feel her pussy pulsate from excitement. Since the day she was raped...Vasthai became more sexually inclined to explore her sexuality. She had been with both men and women. When she married Patrick she tried to give that up.

At this point in time, Vasthai was horny as hell. She wanted some dick and her pussy eaten. Vasthai went to the bed and laid there with her legs spread eagle. In the midst of her fingering her twat, her room door opened.

When she saw who walked into her room, her face lit up with a smile. The two men wasted no time getting down to business. The bald headed one dropped his pants and bent his body enough so that his tongue could taste Vasthai's pussy.

As he was devouring her the second man in the room grabbed his python and placed KY jelly on the head. After he pumped his dick a few times he was rock hard and ready to enter the awaiting piece of ass that was in front of him. He pushed his love inside of the man who was eating Vasthai. Both of the men moaned from the pleasure.

Vasthai had her hands on the man's head that was between her legs. She pushed her clit further in his mouth. She was on the verge of her climax when the man who was eating her; got up and, lunged his dick inside of her.

The two men and Vasthai fucked throughout the night until the early morning. When she woke the next morning Vasthai was alone in her bed still smelling like sex and dick. She planned to relax that day, but when she heard one of the burner cell phones ringing she jumped up to answer it.

"Hello." She said into the receiver as she pulled her naked body from the bed. "Hello, may I speak with Monica." The voice asked on the other end. Vasthai almost told her she had the wrong number; when she remembered she told Layce that her name was Monica.

"This is she. Who's calling?" She asked, already knowing the answer. "Yes, this is Layce Williams. I was calling to let you know, if you wanted to come to the house today, you could. I will have time to give you a proper tour of the house." She said.

"Oh…Layce, from the other day!! The house for sale over on Banderman Drive! I would love to have the tour." Vasthai said as she went to her purse and pulled out her box of Newports.

"If you like, you can stop to the house around three once my husband has left for work." Layce responded to her in a sweet and pleasant tone. Her voice was so sweet and innocent that Vasthai almost had second thoughts of going through with her plans. Then she told herself that Layce was a casualty of war…nothing more and nothing less.

"You have yourself a date! I will be there around three to view your house. Thank you for

calling me. I will you see this afternoon." She said as she hung up the phone.

Vasthai got up and showered. She put on something comfortable, but cute. She fixed her hair, her make-up, and headed out of her hotel room for the remainder of the day.

As she rode to the house she made up her mind to convince Layce to help her in her plans. Vasthai was more than certain that once she saw the package that Layce would be more than willing to comply with the plan.

Vasthai parked three houses down from her destination and popped the trunk of the car. She went in the trunk and retrieved the box with her information it. She opened it and looked for the package was labeled "Layce."

When she found it, she placed the box back in the trunk and walked to the Williams' house. She took a deep breathe and gathered her thoughts before she rang the doorbell. Vasthai waited patiently for her hostess to welcome her.

A few seconds later Layce opened her front door and greeted the woman she knew as Monica. "Good afternoon, Monica!! I am so glad you could make it!" Layce said as she stepped aside and let the woman into the house.

Vasthai looked at the beautiful lady before her and said, "Thank you for allowing me into your house. I am greatly appreciative!!"

Layce led her into the living room as she fixed them a glass of lemonade. Vasthai talked to Layce while she was in the kitchen and she was in the living room. While Layce was in the kitchen

Vasthai observed the many pictures and packed U-Haul moving boxes on the floor.

Layce walked in from the kitchen and sat next to Vasthai. Before Layce could speak again Vasthai interrupted her in mid sentence and said, "Look, Layce my name is Vasthai. I am here because you are going to help me get your husband!!!"

Layce's entire face turned into a scowl. She had let someone into her home that was there under false pretenses, and it was time for the bitch to leave.

"I don't know what the fuck you want, and I could give two fucks less who you are. But you need to get your shit and get out!!!" As she stood up from the sofa she immediately sat back down when she saw pictures of her husband and of herself laying before her on the table.

Layce had not noticed the pictures until she stood up. She picked them up and examined them one by one. What she saw was incriminating evidence of her husband's various affairs committed over the span of their entire relationship. Then she looked at the photos of she and the man she had slept with…a man that was not her husband.

Layce knew about the affairs of her husband. She stayed because she still loved him and because of their daughter Leah. But, when she saw the picture of her husband holding a little boy in his arms, she knew that he was his son.

Layce looked at the many pictures in front of her. She had enough of James' lying and cheating. Layce had made up her mind. She was

down for whatever the plan was and she was going to be a willing participant.

Vasthai knew Layce was on her team. It was now time to fill her in on what the plan was. "This is what we are going to do." Vasthai said as she smiled and made a mental note to move Layce's picture one place forward on the chess board. She was one step closer to check mating the king.

Lights, Camera and Action…Five Days Later

Layce and her daughter Leah were at their new house in Jackson. They were excited because the house was finally complete. Each of them walked around inspecting the house. They had plans on moving some of their things there that upcoming weekend.

Layce and Leah left the house to get some of their things from the old house. They had decided as a family that once the house was completed that they would spend the night there. Little did they know that when they returned they were going to have some uninvited guests.

Vasthai had been following them around for the last few days and was getting her "game face" on. When she saw them leave from the house she waited until the car was out of the subdivision. Vasthai walked up the street and used a copy of the house key to get in.

Once she was in the house she surveyed the home and walked upstairs to what seemed to be the master bedroom. She pulled out one of the cell phone burners from her jacket pocket and called five numbers. She was on the phone for less than

ten minutes. Vasthai told each of them to be at 2512 North Saddleton Street within thirty minutes.

As she waited for her company Vasthai took off her clothes and dressed in all black. She finished off the look with a disposable polypropylene suit, polypropylene shoe covers, and a pair of gloves. She had no intentions of leaving her fingerprints or DNA around that house.

Vasthai went behind herself wiping down the stair banister and the doorknobs when she saw her company walking up to the door. She opened the door and her guests walked hurriedly in the house.

They changed their clothes and put on the provided polypropylene suits and shoe covers that Vasthai had given them. It was 5:32 in the evening. The only thing they could do was wait until they returned.

Two and a half hours later the six of them got quiet when they heard a car pull up in the driveway. It was time!!! Vasthai along with three of her accomplices stood on both sides of the door and waited for it to open. They had their stun guns ready to shoot on contact.

As soon as the key was placed in the door and the first person stepped passed the threshold, the ambush commenced!

James fell to his knees when he felt the immense pain from an 800,000 volt stun gun in his side.

"Ughhh…what is going on?!!" Those were all the words he could utter from his lips before Vasthai hit him again with another electrical shock.

Layce and Leah were grabbed and rushed upstairs where they were both gagged and tied to chairs.

The other three people who were in the house ran upstairs leaving Vasthai alone with her rapist. She looked at him as he lay on the ground trying to recover from the pain. He was weak. Vasthai stood over him and laughed.

"Nigga, you thought you could do what you wanted to people and there would be no repercussions for your actions!!? I have been planning this day for a while and just looking at your punk ass is getting my pussy wet!" She said to him, as her boot came in contact with his ribs.

James was in pain, but, he was coherent. When he heard her voice he knew actually who she was. "Vasthai!! Why are you doing this? Why do you want to hurt my family?" He asked her as he turned to face her. She was not shocked that he was still arrogant. Vasthai bent down, looked him dead in his eyes, and spit in his face.

"You know exactly what you did to me and to your girl Monica!! You are just getting your justly deserved karma...Bitch!" Vasthai was tried of talking and she was ready for him to see what she had in store for him. She pulled out her stun gun and hit him with another volt of electricity. Vasthai demanded that he get his ass up and walk up the stairs.

The walk up the stairs was the longest thing James had ever done in his life. He just knew he was walking into his and his family's death.

When they entered into his new master bedroom he saw what looked to be his wife and

daughter both tied to chairs. The darkness of the room made it difficult for him to positively identify if it was really Layce and Leah in the chairs.

He looked around the room and saw that there were ten people there; six men, Vasthai and his wife and child. He saw that there was a camcorder on a tripod set in the corner and blankets on the floor. James' mind was going a million miles per hour. For the first time he was afraid for his and his family's lives.

Vasthai walked over to Layce and Leah and untied them. She looked at them and saw Layce's eyes showed confusion and fear mixed into one. "The two of you take off all of your clothes!" She told them. Layce looked at her daughter and her eyes told her to do as she was asked.

The two women stripped down to their nakedness. They were as naked as the day they were brought in this world. After they were both done undressing one of the men came and took Leah out of the room. Layce and James were mortified.

"Where are you taking my daughter?" James asked. Vasthai looked at the both of them and did not respond.

Vasthai looked at Layce and said, "Has your husband told you about his past?" Layce shook her head no. Her facial expression said it all. She had no idea what the hell Vasthai was talking about.

She untied her mouth and said to her, "Layce, your husband is a rapist! You see, when I was the same age as your daughter I was a virgin. But, because, your husband couldn't stand the fact

that he was not going to feel the warmth from my pussy, he decided to take it by force! Not only did he take my innocence but he took his mistress' cookies as well! You see, it was only a matter of time before he was going to rape you too!" She said.

Layce looked at her husband. She could not imagine James doing such a thing. "You are lying! He would never do something like that!" She was going to ride or die, right by her man.

Vasthai was not shocked by her response. "Layce you can believe me or not... but your husband fucked me without my permission." With those words she pushed her down on the blankets. Vasthai walked over to the camcorder and pushed record.

"I want you to get your pussy wet!" Vasthai shouted. Layce looked at her as if she was crazy. There was no way she was going to masturbate in front of them. Vasthai had enough of the bullshit. She had paid good money for these men and she was going to get her money's worth.

Vasthai pulled out her nine with the silencer attached to it and told her if she did not do it; she was about to witness the murder of her family. Layce was trapped and had no choice. She closed her eyes and began to touch her breasts. As she started to play in her pussy, Vasthai walked behind James, placed a sock in his mouth, and duct taped his face.

Although, Layce was forced to play with herself, amazingly, she actually started to get into

it!!! They began to hear her juices pop as her fingers moved in and out of her soaking wet twat.

She was so into her masturbation that she did not realize all the men were hovering over her naked body. One of them had his meat in his hand and it was standing at attention. The man dropped his pants and stuck his waiting dick in her pussy.

Layce was not expecting that and she screamed from the pain. One of the other men placed his dick in her mouth while the other man placed his body underneath hers and forced his dick in her ass. Layce had a dick in all of her holes and there was nothing she could do but take it.

James was helpless!!! He could not believe what he was witnessing. He had tears streaming down his cheeks as he watched them deflower his wife in front of him. When he saw Layce throwing it back to the one man who was fucking her pussy he became infuriated. How could she possibly be enjoying herself; James thought to himself.

Vasthai saw the look on his face and walked over to his chair. She slapped him on the back of his head. He was so mesmerized by the events that were taking place in front of him he did not move when he felt the slap.

"I see it on your face!!! You are thinking… how in the fuck she can enjoy this! Let me make it more enjoyable for her!!" She said to James.

Vasthai walked back to the camcorder and shouted, "Let her get on top so she can ride that dick!!" She watched the cracked expression on James' face.

James sat there and watched who he thought was his wife getting fucked by three other men right in front of him. He was thinking about his daughter and where she was. James was praying that they were not raping her like they were raping her mother.

After several hours of watching the men run up in his wife they finally got bored with her. They tied her back up and put her in another room.

James and Vasthai were left alone in the room. She stood in front of his chair and tore off his clothes. He gave her a look of disgust. He wanted to spit in her face, but, he was too weak to do so.

"I have a special treat for you!" She told him as she kissed him on his lips. James just looked at her. In his mind there was nothing she could do to him, but kill him.

Vasthai walked out the room and brought in his daughter, Leah. She looked as if she was crying and her eyes said she was scared. She untied James' mouth so that he could talk.

"If you hurt her I will kill you bitch!!" He said as he looked Vasthai dead in her eyes.

She laughed because he was in no position to make threats. Vasthai told Leah to lie on the blanket. The terrified girl did as she was told. Vasthai stood in front of him and placed her gun in his face.

"No, James I'm about to tell you how this shit is gonna go down!! What you are going to do is fuck your daughter and you are going to enjoy it since you love young virgin pussy!!" She said with a sinister smirk on her face.

James looked at her as if she had lost her fucking mind. "If you think for one moment that I am going to violate my baby, Bitch you got me fucked up!! I may have raped you bitch, but that was personal!!!" He shouted at her.

Vasthai was not fazed by what he said because she knew he was going to do what she wanted. She knew that James' ego was not going to allow him to be killed by a woman.

"I'll tell you what!!! If you don't do what I'm telling you to do, those three men who just finished fucking your wife will fuck her!! But, this time she will not enjoy it!! I will personally make sure that they use foreign objects to ram in that pussy of hers!! Those objects are going to go so deep inside of her…I promise you…the bitch will never have kids or want to fuck another day in her life!! After all of that, I am going to take your precious Leah, find the first male dog in heat, and let him fuck her doggie style! Once I had all of my laughs I will kill her and send her remains to you! Sweetie, the choice is yours!!!" Vasthai blurted out to him still holding her gun.

James was stuck between a rock and hard spot. His tears flooded his eyes. He could not bring himself to fuck his daughter, but he did not want them fucking her either. Let alone doing something to her to make her barren and couldn't have children. He was stuck.   "Alright, just give me a minute to get my mind right!!" It was then Vasthai saw that he was willing to do what he could to protect his seed, even if it meant doing some foul shit.

Vasthai was standing in the corner watching James take away what he thought was Leah's prized possession. As she watched him, she saw visions of him violating her when she was that age. Although, she knew it was sick, but her pussy was dripping from seeing him take his daughter.

In her mind, she was damaging the one who turned her into a person who was bitter and vengeful. If James thought this was his only punishment, then he was mistaken. This was only act one of the game plan.

Vasthai directed James as he fucked and raped his daughter. She told him to fuck her as if she was his personal porn star. With those words said, James went to work. He wanted to make his performance look authentic.

James was so humiliated by what he was doing that he did not notice the girl he was fucking didn't have his daughter's birthmark on the inside of her left thigh. It was the same birthmark that Layce had on her inner thigh as well. He was so distraught and heartbroken that he even missed the tattoo on her body.

James pushed his love inside of Leah and contorted her body in sexual positions she had no idea about. Leah was in her own world. She was confused as to what her body was feeling. Her father was having sex with her but her pussy was feeling good. Before she knew what happened a loud moan escaped from her mouth. Everyone in the room except James laughed. They all knew she just had her first orgasm.

When James heard Leah's moans of ecstasy he became furious. In his moment of rage he violently slapped his daughter. When he struck her she was in shock. "Why did you slap me daddy?" She asked him. He looked at her and went crazy.

"So you like this shit!! How can you cum when you're getting fucked by your father!! IF you want to be a motherfucking woman...I'm gonna to fuck you like one!!" He could not understand how she was enjoying this experience.

For the next hour James fucked his daughter as if she was a stranger. He fucked her, made her suck his dick, and swallow his nut. When he was ready to cum he busted inside of her; making sure her body accepted every drop.

Vasthai was satisfied with his performance. When they were finished she told Leah to go into the other room where her mother was. They had been in the house for almost twenty-four hours and she was running out of time.

Guilty Until Proven Innocent
Chapter 13

James and his family were left in their home with no clothes and no car. However, Vasthai left them a burner and told them she would be calling them. The three of them were exhausted and confused by their ordeal. Finally, Layce was able to calm their daughter down enough to get her to go to sleep.

Layce was glad she was asleep because she needed to have a private conversation with her husband. Layce closed the room door to where Leah was and walked to the next room where James was. When she walked in the room she saw James standing on the wall.

"We need to talk!! IS IT TRUE... DID YOU RAPE HER!!?" She asked him as she walked and planted herself in front of him.

James did not want to have this conversation with her. He was still fucked up about taking his daughter's virginity. "Look, Layce this is not the time for this shit!! Have we not all been through enough for one day!?" He said never looking at her.

Layce was dumbfounded. She could not believe he felt this was an inappropriate time to have this conversation. She needed to know...was he the reason why this happened to her and her

daughter? "James... I promise you this...if you don't start talking I am going to kill you!! Nigga don't test me because you will not win this battle!!" She said.

James finally took his eyes off the wall and looked at his wife. When he looked into her eyes he saw she was dead serious about killing him. He had no more fight in him and if she tried to kill him he probably would not have fought back.

"Look that shit happened a long time ago!! I was young, dumb, and made some mistakes! But I never did anything to deserve this; to have my wife raped or to have to fuck my daughter!!" Without openly saying he was guilty, James was confessing to his accused crime.

"So let me get this straight!! You raped someone and you think you don't deserve some revenge!! You have destroyed that woman's being and because of your dick...my daughter and I have had to pay for your sins!!" Layce was so enraged by hearing those words leave her lips that she saw red.

Before James had time to react Layce kicked him so hard in his "Johnson" that he dropped to the floor screaming and holding his dick. Layce went to the door and locked it. She had no intentions of letting her daughter walk in on this ass whipping she was about to give him.

Layce walked back over to James and got on the ground where he was still in pain holding himself. She grabbed his head and began to bang it against the floor.   "You motherfucker!! This is your fucking fault!!! You raped her and my

daughter... and you think you did nothing wrong!!"
She shouted at him.

James was in double pain. He was getting his head beat in and his dick was throbbing. James pleaded for her to stop. When her arms got tired from banging his head on the floor; Layce got up and stomped him repeatedly in his dick with her foot. IF she had a weapon she would have pulled the trigger and ended his misery.

While she was administering as much pain as she could to her husband; she heard the burner ringing. Layce quickly picked up the phone and listened for the voice on the other end to speak.

"There will be a car at the house to pick the three of you up in the next twenty-four hours." The voice informed her. She never had a chance to ask questions because the line went dead.

Layce was left to her thoughts as she sat in the corner watching James hold his dick in pain. Her mind was confused. She had been with James for sixteen years and married to him for two. In all of this time, she never would have guessed James was capable of rape.

James gathered what little strength he had left and grabbed his wife's hand. Layce felt his touch, but she never wanted him to touch her again. As she pushed his hand away, she made up in her mind that if she survived this ordeal that she and Leah were gone. She could not spend one more second with a man who raped her daughter and another woman.

Layce had time to think back on her life with James and she was blinded by the warning

signs. She was seventeen when she brought James to meet her mother. Her mother was very leery of James from the first moment she met him.

Layce who was head strong and new to Mississippi knew little about James but her mother was determined to find out as much information about the new boy that had befriended her daughter as possible. Stacy was young when she had Layce and she sent her to stay with her eldest sister in Ohio.

When Stacy had turned thirty-three she sent for her daughter to come and finish her last year of high school with her in Jackson, Mississippi.

Stacy who was known to have her hand in various hustles went to the streets to gather information on the twenty-two year old James. What she heard from reliable sources was not what she wanted to hear. Stacy found out information about James and immediately informed her daughter.

Layce had tears coming from her eyes as she remembered the conversation between her and her mother about James.

"Layce, look, I know you resent me for not raising you and for sending you to your aunt. I was young and had no idea of how to be a mother. Now if you can give me a chance we can build a strong relationship between us. I know you think I don't want to see you happy, but your happiness is all that I am living for."

Layce sat looking at her mother as if she was crazy. She had some fucking nerve to be trying to be motherly. *"Mom, I know that you are*

concerned about me seeing James, but James is just my friend for right now! I'm seventeen and still a virgin! So if you are trying to have the sex talk with me you can save that sh..."

Layce never had a chance to get the words from her mouth. Her mother slapped her so hard in the mouth that she fell over in the chair she was sitting in. *"Let me tell your motherfuckin ass one thing! I don't give a fuck if my sister raised you! You are my child and I will kill your ass if you ever...ever...ever talk to me that way again!! For your information James was sent to Mississippi to live with his brother after he got into some trouble with a girl!! He has been hiding here because the nigga has a bounty on his head. If he is caught alive again in Georgia that's his ass!! All that I am saying to you is, you need to be careful!"*

Layce was hell bent on rebelling against her mother. She never took heed to her mother's words. She continued to see James, eventually married him, and had a baby from him. Now, after all these years she wished she would have listened or at least investigated her mother's claims. If she had dug a little she would have heard from the streets that James was known for forcing his dick in "virgin pussy."

Time for the Shit to hit the fan

Vasthai had less than three hours before her hired help was to pick up James and his family. She had to make a few more stops before she headed to the airport.   She had spent the last several hours editing the home porno of James and his daughter;

now Vasthai was heading to drop the last copy of the DVD off to it's respective place.

Vasthai had everything in place for part two of her plan. She could not wait to see the outcome. Her last stop was to see Tyrone before she caught her flight. As she drove the thirty minute drive back to the prison she listened to the Tom Joyner Morning Show. Vasthai laughed her ass off as she listened to Tom, Sybil, and J. Anthony Brown.

The sun had barely risen in the East when she walked into the prison and was escorted directly to Tyrone's cell. He was awakened when he heard his cell door open. When he opened his eyes he saw what he thought was his mother standing in the tiny cell.

"Tyrone, wake up baby." Vasthai said to her son. Tyrone sat up on his hard bed and faced his mother.   "Mom, what are you doing here? How are you even allowed in my cell?" He asked her as he fixed his eyes on her face.

"Don't worry about how I'm able to see you up close and personal. I want to tell you that I love you. Soon you will know the whole truth and you will be home." She said as she bent down and kissed her son on his cheek.

"What are you talking about…coming home? Shit I got a twenty year bid! There is no way that I will be home anytime soon." Tyrone stood and faced his mother. Vasthai did not acknowledge his words and kissed him again. She smiled and told him that she loved him again and turned to walk out the cell.

Tyrone went to the closed bars and watched his mother walk down the cell block corridor. He was at a lost for words. He sat back down on his bed and got his thoughts together. Tyrone played back in his mind the entire time that he spent with his mother.

"Man, what the fuck is going on! This shit makes no sense! How in the fuck was my mother able to see me alone for hours with no CO? How was she able to walk in my cell?!!" He said to himself out loud.

Tyrone had no answers for his questions but he knew that she had to have put in some favors to do all of the above. It was almost 6:30 in the morning and he was unable to go back to sleep. He went to his sink and brushed his teeth and washed his face. After he took care of his hygiene Tyrone went into his daily exercise routine of sit-ups and push-ups.

It was 7:30 in the morning when Monica turned on her television to the local morning news. What she saw on the news made her drop her coffee on her kitchen floor. She went to her living room and turned the volume up to hear what the news reporter was saying. As she watched the broadcast she heard the phone that Vasthai had given her ringing.

Monica rushed to her purse and quickly answered the phone. "Hello." She said into the receiver. "Are you watching the news?" Vasthai asked her.

"What have you done? I am standing here watching what looks to be a tape of James fucking an underage girl!!!" She replied.

"Look, don't worry about what I did. It's time for you to do your end of the deal. I sent you a little gift just to ensure that you keep your word. When you leave the house you will see your gift." Vasthai said as she hung the phone up.

Monica hung up the phone and walked to her front door. She opened her front door and saw a manila envelope sitting on her doorstep. She looked around to see if anyone saw her pick up the envelope. Monica retrieved the package and turned to walk back in the house.

Monica sat on her sofa, opened the manila envelope, and found a handwritten note addressed to her inside another envelope. She took the note and opened the neatly folded paper to read. She almost lost her breakfast when she opened the other envelope. Monica went through the house until she located her magnifying eyeglass.

When she placed her eye through the glass and examined the photo negatives she could feel the vomit in her throat. Monica did everything in her power to prevent her food from coming back up. She thought no one knew about how she got her promotion to DA. Now, here she was looking at concrete proof that you could never hide from your past.

Vasthai had managed to find out about her and the judge fucking. Now she was holding that information over her to ensure that she would comply with her plan.

Monica had all intentions of doing her part of the plan but now she had no choice but to fulfill her end. She carried the negatives back to her bedroom and placed them in her dresser drawer. Monica gathered her things and headed out the door to work.

Turning the Tables
Chapter 14

It was exactly 8:30 in the morning when a man walked into the house where James, Layce and Leah were waiting for him to take them to their home on Banderman Drive. He slowly walked up the stairs with clothes in his hands.

James heard someone climbing the stairs as he woke his wife and daughter up from their sleep. The man entered the room never saying a word. He handed them their respective clothes and walked back out of the door.

The three of them quickly dressed and ran down the stairs taking them two at a time. When they opened the front door there was a limo waiting for them. An older white man was there at the door holding it open for them to enter. "Where is the man who entered the house?" James asked the man.

The man looked confused because he had not seen anyone. "Sir, I was paid to pick up the Williams' family and drive them to an address on Banderman Drive. I have not seen this man that you are speaking of." He said as he stepped out of the way for them to enter into the back of the limo.

James and his family were mentally and physically tired. They did not have the energy to ask questions. One by one they got into the limo and rode in silence to their home.

The man who they were looking for was sitting behind the wheel of a parked car. They were not able to see him because he was slumped down in the driver's seat undetected from view. As the limo drove away he placed a call and drove away from the curb.

When the limo approached the street of its intended destination, James noticed that there were two police cars posted in front of his home. He was concerned because he thought the house had been broken into.

As the limo got closer to the house; James realized that the police were standing in front of the house as if they were waiting for them. "What the fuck is going on?" He said out loud.

The limo stopped and the driver headed for the back door to open it. When the three of them exited the limo the driver drove off leaving the Williams' family to face their fate with the law.

Monica who was there with the police walked up to James, Layce, and Leah and said, "Mr. James Williams, I have a warrant for your arrest." As she proceeded to recite his Miranda rights to him, James was flabbergasted at what was happening.

He had no idea what the fuck was going on. To make matters worse his ex-mistress was there face to face with his wife.

"What are you talking about!!!??? Where are you taking my husband??" Layce protested as she and her daughter watched the police officer place handcuffs on James. Monica and Layce

looked at each other and locked eyes. They looked at each other as if they were enemies.

Monica knew she was inches from the wife of the man who was not long ago in her bed. Little did she know, Layce already knew who she was and she was not even tripping about Monica fucking her husband.

James chose to remain silent and did not resist arrest. The two officers led him to the awaiting squad car and proceeded to take him to the jail. James hoped that his wife found it in her heart to call their lawyer Kennedy and have her meet him at the precinct.

Once Layce saw the car take her husband away she sent Leah inside of the house. As Leah walked inside the house Monica turned around to leave when she heard her name come from Layce's mouth.

Monica was stunned by the revelation that she knew who she was. That meant one thing; that she knew she had been sleeping with her husband. Layce walked to where Monica was and the two women looked at each other once more.

Although, the temperature was hot outside the look in the two women's eyes was cold. Layce took a deep breath and said, "I know that you have been fucking my husband. If the circumstances were different trust and believe, I would have placed my size eight so far in that tight ass of yours, that you would have had to beg and plead with me to stop fucking you in your ass!!!!"

Monica studied the woman before her. She saw in her demeanor that she was done with her

husband. What bothered her was...how she even knew about the affair between her and James? "I see that you are a bitter woman. Does it bother you that I fucked your husband? Or should I say...I fucked him as he laid in my bed on many nights lying to you about where he really was. Of course he was with me in my bed with his head in my pussy and not with you." Monica said back to Layce with the same venom that Layce had spewed from her own mouth.

Layce stepped so close to Monica's face that she could feel her breathing on her nose. "Let me tell you something honey, if I were you, I wouldn't brag about fucking a married man. That admission only makes you look like a high priced pitiful whore. It makes you look even sillier because from what I understand, you were the one crazy in love with a nigga who was never going to leave his home. Sweetie, I want to thank you for taking him off my hands. With trash like that sticking his dick in whatever hole; I can do better. So thank you for setting me free. When I am done with him you can have him because I have already used him all up!!!" Layce said.

The two women stared at each other for another few seconds. They both understood each other. It was true, Monica was in love with James, but she could never be with him again after what he did to her. It was equally true that Layce loved her husband, but Vasthai had given her a way out of her marriage. The two women walked away from each other, going in different directions.

As Monica and Layce walked away from each other, Vasthai sat in her plush first class airplane seat watching the two women. She had more than one laugh to last her a lifetime.

Vasthai was able to watch the verbal catfight via her burner cell phone. The unsuspecting women were being watched by a closed circuit television that had been strategically placed in the light post directly in front of Layce and James' house.

Vasthai was pleased that her manipulation of both Monica and Layce was working well in her favor. What neither of them knew was that she had gone to them both separately, convinced them that it was in their best interest to work with her and not against her.

For Layce she would be free to walk away from a man who not only continuously fucked around on her, but also had a child from another woman and concealed it.

For Monica she would have the chance to see the man who rejected and raped her suffer a fate that was fitting for a man who had everything to lose and nothing to gain.

As for Vasthai she would be seeking closure to a part of life that had kept her in bondage for far too long.

The Chess Game Thickens....
Chapter 15

James was escorted into the jail. It was the same jail in which he once escorted convicts to their own jail cells. Now he was facing the same fate of jail time. He remained silent and never said a word to any of the police's questions. They should have known that he was just as familiar with the law as they were. Although, he was not one of them he went by their same code.

He waited until he was able to make his phone call. James was not about to wait for Layce to call their attorney. He was in trouble and he needed his legal defense present representing him.

"Thank you for calling Curry, Jacobson and Scott Law firm. How may I direct your call?" James heard the receptionist say when he called to speak with his lawyer.

"I need to speak with Kennedy Scott." He told the pleasant woman on the other end of the line. As he was waiting for his call to be transferred to Kennedy, James was praying that she was available to speak with him. His mind was drifting to what he was being charged with.

He heard Kennedy come to the line and say, "This is Kennedy Scott. How can I help you?"

James was so relieved when he heard her voice, "Kennedy this is James Williams. I need you to come downtown to the jail. I am under arrest and they have not told me on what charge." He said all in one winded breath. Kennedy listened intently on the other end of the phone. She had been waiting for this call.

Two days prior to James' arrest she saw the woman who she called almost three years ago, walking through her office door. This was the first time she had laid eyes on the woman named Vasthai, who was named in James' psychiatrist's notes. When she first met with Rodney she inquired about her and wanted to know what his diagnosis of James was.

Rodney, who was the police and correctional officer's psychiatrist, told Kennedy that he thought James was a narcissistic psychopath who raped woman not because of the pussy, but because of the power he possessed over them when he was committing the act. From what she gathered from Rodney, James was advised to see him when he flipped out at work and had a temporary mental breakdown.

"James, I will be there within the hour. Don't say a word without me present!!!" Kennedy said to her client as she hung up the phone.

Kennedy sat in her leather chair and looked blankly at the wall. She had agreed to help Vasthai under two conditions. Kennedy asked Vasthai to bring her mother to Mississippi. Her second request of Vasthai was for her not to ask what her

motivations were for wanting to help her take down James.

Kennedy gathered her belongings and headed out of her office. She stopped at her personal receptionist's desk and told her that she would be gone for the rest of the day.

Kennedy strutted to the elevator. As she walked to the elevator she heard the burner cell phone that Vasthai had given her beep.

She retrieved the phone from her purse and read the new text message. The message said *I am here.... Send me the address.* Kennedy quickly responded to the text and but in the address that was requested from her. Kennedy could feel the adrenaline racing through her veins. She put her game face on because it was now time to put her agenda aside and defend her guilty client.

James sat in the jail cell and waited patiently for Kennedy to arrive. It had been over an hour and he still had not been pulled out of the cell to confer with his legal counsel. He still had no idea what charge he was being held on. James was sitting in a crowded cell with other men who were there waiting for transport or waiting for their arraignment hearings.

James decided to sit in the corner by himself so he could think. As he was sat in his seat the midday news came on the television that was on the wall on the outside of the cell.

The newscast caught his attention when he read the caption across the screen that said, *"Anonymous DVD of a man having sex with what appears to be an under-aged girl."* The caption also

said, *"That the clip that they were about to air could be inappropriate for viewers under the age of thirteen."*

James felt a chill run up the back of his spine. He was feeling the guilt of how he violated his own daughter. James had to keep telling himself that he did what he did in order for his family to survive.

James' eyes widened when he saw the clip of the DVD. He literary had to swallow the vomit that was in his throat. He felt the sweat trickling down his forehead as he watched before his eyes... the DVD of him fucking his daughter. He was sick!!!

As he tried to compose himself...he could feel the stares of the other men glaring in his direction. James knew if Kennedy did not arrive soon that he was about to have to fight!!

He knew that he had to act fast before one of other inmates tried him and a physical altercation popped off."Nigga...what fuck are you looking at!!!??" He said speaking directly to the main man who was mugging him from the other side of the cell.

The man who he was directly spewing his venom looked at James and said, "I am looking at your pussy stealing, child molesting ass!!! Nigga...fuck with me if you want... I got something for bitch ass!!!" The man said as he positioned his body closer to the center of the cell so he could show James that it was nothing if he wanted to go toe to toe with him.

James saw that he was going to have to fuck ole boy up. In jail, regardless if it was county, state, or the federal penal system it was survival of the fittest and if you were perceived as weak then you were fucked!!! James prepared to handle his lightweight when the officer came to the cell and called out, "Williams...your lawyer is here!"

He casually walked past his adversary and looked at him with contempt. He turned around with his back to the officer and allowed him to handcuff him. When the officer was done securing his hands, the two of them walked silently to the client/lawyer room.

As the two of them walked to the room, James thought to himself...the words of the Jay-Z song: *It was all good just a week ago.* Oh how his situation had changed for the worse!!! To make matters worse, if he told the truth about what happened to him and his family; he would surely be convicted of whatever charge he was being accused of.

James walked into the room and sat across from Kennedy and waited to hear what she had to tell him. His gut told him that he was fucked!!! But for some reason his instincts also told him that he had been set up for his own down fall.

The only thing that he could hope for was that Kennedy was as good of a lawyer as everyone had told him she was.

Word Travels Fast
Chapter 16

Tyrone was eating lunch with his clique of inmates when one of them said, "Yo...y'all hear about Williams?" He stated as he placed the cardboard tasting food into his mouth. They all heard the rumors, but none of them knew if they were true.

The inmates were silent for a few minutes as they consumed their meal. Tyrone looked at his boys and said, "Y'all think his black ass is going to get locked down with us? I mean the DVD of him could be a fabrication. I mean he could go the R. Kelly route and say it wasn't him!!!" They all laughed but stopped when they heard one of the COs coming over to the table telling them that lunch was over.

The four men rose from their seats with the trays in their hands and emptied their food in the trash. Each man in the prison was talking about the scandal. Everyone had their own opinion and theory about what really happened.

As for Tyrone, he sympathized with Williams. It was not long ago that he too was accused of raping a woman. Now, the CO, just as Tyrone had would have to face the jury and his fate.

Tyrone's one hope was that while he was incarcerated that he would be truly rehabilitated for his crime. What he knew for sure was, if

Williams was coming to prison, he better prepare himself for the worst!!!

The word had already gotten around and there were two kinds of inmates that were killed on the regular....rapists and child molesters.

Ghosts from the Past...
Chapter 17

Vasthai finished watching the fiasco that she had created; then placed the burner back in her purse. She sat the rest of the plane ride absorbed in her thoughts. Before she got on her flight she received a text from both Monica and Layce saying that James was placed under arrest.

She could not do anything but laugh at the situation because it was all too funny to her. Vasthai's plan was going all to well. It was going so well that she felt something was going to go wrong.

She looked inside her Fendi purse and pulled out a folder that contained her most valuable commodity... information. As she looked over all the information she had on each of her pawns in her chess game, she put the rest of the information back in her purse when she came to Kennedy's info.

There was not much she could find out about her. What information she did have about her was vague. The only concrete information Vasthai knew about Kennedy was that she graduated from Howard Law with honors. She never married and every relationship she had always ended because she would never let down her emotional walls.

As far as her childhood there was no information. It was as if everything about her from birth up until she graduated from Howard was expunged from existence.

When she walked into Kennedy's office to speak with her about what she wanted her to do; Vasthai got the distinct feeling that she had been waiting for her. It was as if she knew that they would meet one day.

Vasthai had agreed to her two requests. She needed her on her team and she was not about to fuck up all she had put into motion because she was unwilling to compromise.

"I need to find out what her motivation is for so willingly wanting to go along with the program." Vasthai said to herself as she heard the pilot saying that they were landing and to put their seatbelts on.

She walked off the plane and headed straight to the awaiting limo that was parked in front of the airport. Vasthai had no luggage because she only planned to be in the city overnight. When she got into the back seat of the limo she rolled down the partition window and told the driver she was going to 5550 West Infinity Drive Lane.

As she rode in the limo she decided that she wanted to talk to her husband. She reached inside of her purse, pulled out her BlackBerry, and dialed her house number. The phone rang three times before Patrick picked up saying, "Hello."

"Hey baby how are you doing? I miss you!!" She said sweetly in the phone. "Hey there. I miss you too!! When are you coming home? Kamron and Tyson keep asking me when you are coming back." Patrick said as he put on his Cole and Hann shoes.

Vasthai was quiet on the phone. She told her husband she was only going to be in Mississippi for a week, but it had been over a month, since then.

Her timeframe was three months to enact and see her plan to fruition. She could not leave with her chess game not finished... she needed to checkmate.

"I know baby. But you know that I don't get to see Tyrone often. I just want to spend a little more time with him. Actually, I was thinking about coming home and bringing daddy down here to see him too." Vasthai told her husband as she felt the limo coming to a stop.

"Patrick, I know that Kamron and Tyson are both in school right now. You tell my other babies that I love them and I will call them tonight. I have to call you back. I am running late to see Tyrone. I love you boo!!!" She said to Patrick as the driver came to her door and held it open for her.

Before Patrick could tell his wife that he loved her back the phone line disconnected. He and Vasthai had been together since she was eighteen years old and he knew that she was up to something. Vasthai thought that he didn't know about the box that she kept at her father's house.

He sat on their bed and decided that he would give his frat brother a call and inquire about his co-worker, James Williams. What Vasthai didn't know was that he too was keeping tabs on her rapist and his son's biological father.

Vasthai stepped out of the open limo door and walked slowly to the front door of the house. She walked on the porch and listened to see if she heard voices. After a few minutes of listening she knocked on the door and waited for someone to answer.

Phoenix had just snorted the last of the cocaine she had. She had not even had the opportunity to enjoy her high because she heard the knock at the door.

"Who the fuck could that be at the door???" She said to herself hoping that whoever it was would go away so she could enjoy her high.

As Phoenix settled her head back on the pillow that was on the couch she heard the person knock again at the door. This time she became irritated, stood up, walked to the door, and swung it open. "What the fuck do you want!!?" She said to the lady who stood before her on her porch.

Vasthai looked at the woman who she had agreed to deliver back to Mississippi, ignored her comment, and quickly pushed Phoenix to the side as she entered the house.

Phoenix turned around and looked at the woman as if she had lost her ever-loving mind. The woman had definitely blown her high. Before Phoenix could spit her venom at the woman, she felt the pain of the stun gun that Vasthai held in her hand.

Phoenix was going down from the pain of the stun gun. The woman who administered the pain grabbed her before she hit the hardwood floor. Vasthai quickly placed Phoenix back on the couch and swiftly moved to close and lock the door.

Vasthai sat in front of the woman who she only knew as Kennedy's mother. She lit up one of her Newports and waited for the shock of the stun gun to leave from the woman's body. Phoenix was finally able to compose herself.

The two women looked at each other, both sizing the other up. Vasthai handed the woman one of her cigarettes and she eagerly took the cancer stick and placed it in her mouth. She handed her the lighter that was in her hand and she lit up the cigarette.

Vasthai broke the silence and said to the woman, "Look, I am not here to hurt you. I was sent here by someone to take you back with me to Mississippi. I don't even know your name…so let's start this meeting with a clean slate!!! I apologize for using the stun gun on you…my name is Vasthai. What is your name?"

When Phoenix heard the word Mississippi her heart immediately wailed with overwhelming grief. She thought of the daughter that she had not seen in over two years. Phoenix had refused to see her daughter for two specific reasons. The first reason was that she had become a full blown addict, and the second reason was that she felt too much shame when she looked at her.

Although, it was not Kennedy's fault as to how she was conceived; the pain that was associated with her conception was too much for her to bear. Phoenix knew Kennedy had found out the truth when she overheard her mother and her grandmother arguing. She always wanted to tell Kennedy herself. She didn't want her to hear it from two women having that conversation in a heated confrontation.

"Who sent you here? How do I know that you won't kill me?" Phoenix knew that the life she was living was one of treachery and she could lose

her life if she let her guard down. Vasthai could see the fear and uncertainty in her eyes. She needed to calm her apprehension.

"Look, I don't even know what your name is!!! All Kennedy asked me to do, was come here, and bring her mother back to the Magnolia State. Trust and believe you are coming with me one way or the other. So let's stop the bullshit!!! So that we are clear, I have no intentions of doing any harm to you as long as you don't do anything stupid!!" Vasthai told her as she walked over to where Phoenix was sitting and sat next to her on the couch.

The two women once again looked at each other. Phoenix felt better knowing that her daughter was behind her kidnapping and not someone who had placed a hit on her. "My daughter didn't tell you my name?" She asked as she finished the last of the cigarette.

"No, I did not ask her. She and I made an agreement that I would not ask her about her motivations for wanting to help me out. I will say this though; we have to get you cleaned up so you can kick this monkey off your back." Vasthai responded as she held the small compact mirror up with the small trace amount of the narcotic on it.

"My name is Phoenix and I am sorry that you had to meet me under these conditions. I was not always this way. I get high so I can forget the things in my life that I want to erase. Being high numbs my pain and takes me to a place where I don't have to face the truth. The truth is that my life

is fucked!!!" She confessed as a single tear rolled down the side of her face.

Vasthai felt her pain because there had been plenty of times through her life that she wanted to do nothing more than to numb the brokenness that was in her life. The only thing that helped her to keep it together was her husband and children.

"I am gonna keep it real with you. Phoenix, I don't know what has happened in your life. But, it's time for you to pick your ass up and try to move on past the hurt. Now, I am not saying to forget because you will never forget what or who has caused you to fall from your peace and sanity. You have to be a strong bitch and save your energy for making yourself whole." Vasthai said.

Vasthai pulled Phoenix up by her arm and led her to the bathroom. She started the shower and made sure that it was piping hot. Once the water was hot and the mirror was fogged she stepped out of the bathroom to let Phoenix handle her hygiene.

As Phoenix was in the shower Vasthai took it upon herself to inspect her surroundings. She walked around the house and noticed that the house was nicely furnished and everything was in its place.

Vasthai knew she had to move quickly so she would not be detected in her snooping. She walked into the master bedroom. In one quick glance she took in everything in the room and where it was located. Vasthai went to the dresser and pulled out the drawer that appeared to be the underwear one.

She ran her hands underneath the panties and felt something that felt like a picture. Vasthai retrieved the item, placed it close to her face, and examined it. The picture looked like it was Phoenix, her parents, and her brother. Vasthai looked on the back of the picture and written on the back was "family vacation."

She quickly placed the picture back and her hand felt something else. She pulled out what looked to be an official document. When she opened the document she realized that it was Kennedy's birth certificate.

Vasthai didn't have a chance to fully read the document because she heard the shower head turning off in the bathroom.

Vasthai quickly pulled out one of the burners from her pocket and snapped a picture of the birth certificate. She heard Phoenix in the bathroom brushing her teeth. As Phoenix brush her teeth and gargled her mouth with mouthwash she put the paper back in its place and hurried back in the living room.

Phoenix got dressed and the two women headed out the door. She took nothing with her, but the clothes on her back and her purse. They walked to the waiting limo and were escorted in by the limo driver.

Before they headed back to the airport, they drove to the spot where Phoenix got her drugs from. Phoenix hurried to her usual dealer and copped what she needed and headed back to the limo. Once back in limo they drove to the Chocolate Factory restaurant to eat.

When they entered the restaurant Phoenix rushed to the ladies room so she could consume her drug of choice and enjoy the high she was suppose to have had before she and Vasthai had their encounter.

When she returned from the bathroom the two of them placed their orders, made small talk, and waited to be served. Their flight was not scheduled to leave until 11pm so they had some time to get to know each other.

Kennedy waited in the room that was provided for attorney/client conferences. She pulled out the information and DVD that she had from her briefcase. As she pulled the items from her briefcase she saw the CO bringing James in the room and over to the table where she was.

Kennedy stood to her feet and extended her hand to shake her client's. The two exchanged pleasantries and took their seat. She spoke first and said, "Look, James I am going to cut straight to the chase. There is some damning evidence against you. I need for you to tell me how you got into this mess. I need for you to tell me the truth!!! I don't give a fuck how fucked up it might be. In order for me to prepare an adequate defense I have to hear your side of the story." She told him leading him to believe that she had his best interest at heart.

James leaned back in his chair to let the words of his lawyer penetrate through his mind. He was contemplating whether or not to tell her the truth about the DVD. He knew that he had to help himself. He hadn't even seen his wife and began to

wonder if she had deserted him when he needed her the most.

Kennedy's BlackBerry rang snapping James from his thoughts. Kennedy answered the phone and after answering "yes" to the person on the other end, she stood up, walked around to where James was, and placed the phone to his ear.

James looked at her with a look of confusion. Kennedy told him that it was Layce on the phone. Suddenly, there was a smile on his face. He quickly said, "Hello" and was relieved when he heard his wife's voice on the other end.

"Baby, how are you? I called Kennedy but she had informed me that you had already called her. I will be there as soon as possible. Has she already told you that she is trying to get a bail hearing for you?" She said to her husband.

"I am holding up in here. I was starting to think that you left a nigga for dead! I just got in here with Kennedy and we hadn't had the chance to discuss the case yet." He told her.

Layce listened to James speak. She already knew Kennedy was there with him. The only reason why she called was to tell him to tell Kennedy about what happened and to make him feel that she had not abandoned him.

When Layce called Vasthai and told her about James' arrest, Vasthai asked Layce to call him and encourage him to tell his lawyer about the escapade they had endured. As she pretended to listen to her husband her mind went back to the house where it all went down. Layce actually had to conceal the laughter that was building inside her.

The crime that he was being accused of was not what it seemed.

"Look, baby I know that you may not want to, but I think that you have to tell Kennedy what happened at the house!!! I mean she is your lawyer and whatever you tell her will be kept confidential."

James heard his wife's words and it was at that moment he knew he had nothing to lose. He had to tell her. "Look, I want to see you soon. Let me get off the phone so we can start this conference. Layce, I love you and I am sorry for all of the wrong I have done to you." He told his wife as he moved his face from the phone indicating that he was done talking.

Kennedy placed the phone to her ear and she and Layce talked for another minute before hanging up. Kennedy was starting to feel a certain degree of vindication when she saw that James was sick with fear as to what the fate of his future was.

She picked up the conversation where she left off before the phone rang. Kennedy held the infamous DVD up in her hand and said, "I don't know if you had the chance to watch the news, but this is the District Attorney's smoking gun. This was hand delivered to all of the local news stations. I even think that one was sent over night to the CNN station in Atlanta. This is going to kill us if you don't tell me who has it in for you and even if this DVD is authentic." She said as she pulled out her box of cigarettes and handed one to him.

Although, James had stopped smoking over a year ago he needed something to calm his nerves. They both inhaled the nicotine from their cigarettes.

"The DVD is me, but I had no choice!!! I had to commit this act in order to save the lives of my wife and daughter. I am going to tell you the truth. I know who is behind all of this drama in my life... a bitch named Vasthai!!!" He said with the bass in his voice of a man who knew that the cards were stacked against him.

Kennedy pulled out her pen to take notes. She wanted to hear exactly what her accomplice did to him. "I'm sorry. I don't quite follow you. What do you mean Vasthai is behind this? Who is this person that you are referring too?" She asked as she intently listened to what he had to say.

James leaned over the table and in a whisper said, "When I was younger, I did things that I now regret. I mean, I was a boy who didn't take rejection well and things just got out of control. Now, many years later I am reaping what I have sewn. I need your word that whatever I tell you, you will not be use against me, because what I am about to tell you may implicate me in past crimes."

Kennedy confirmed that whatever was said to her was protected under lawyer/client privilege and she could lose her license to practice law if she disclosed what was discussed between them.

When James felt completely comfortable he purged his soul to her. He took her all the way back before the rape of Vasthai to a rape of someone they both knew all to well. He brought her up to the present with all of his many affairs; to the son he had with one of his mistresses, up to the events that took place in his new home.

When Kennedy was done with her session with James she was extremely upset, because he blatantly admitted to what she knew was the truth. His confession only gave her more of a motivation to make sure that she went through with what she was doing.

On the way out of the county jail Kennedy pulled out her TracPhone and called Rodney. She needed to ask him a question. The phone rang three times before he picked up.

"Lawyer, tell me something good!" He said into the phone. "Hey, I need to ask you a quick question. At anytime did James tell you anything about a rape that he committed before he raped Vasthai?" She asked.

Rodney thought their business was done and he no longer wanted to be involved with whatever she was doing. He had already decided that he was leaving the city and starting anew. Rodney had plans on calling his frat brother and asking him for help in getting a job working in the hospital where he worked.

"Kennedy, I think our business is done. If you are not calling me for an appointment then there is nothing for us to discuss!!!" He told her, as he was about to press the end button on his cell.

"Rodney, I will pay you another 50k for your information. Just meet me at the usual spot so we can talk. Once you have given me the info that I am requesting, I will never bother you again." She told him as she hung up the phone, got in her car, and drove over to the bar.

The Flight Back to Mississippi

Vasthai and Phoenix boarded the plane and settled into their first class seats. Phoenix made sure she was high enough so she would not be sick on the short flight.

What Vasthai didn't know was when Phoenix was extremely high she was a chatter-box. She had endured her talking about what seemed to be nothing. She really didn't pay attention to what Phoenix was saying until she mentioned having been sent away for telling the truth about her brother.

Vasthai wanted to know everything and she planned on getting as much info from Phoenix as she could before she was delivered to her daughter.

"What do you mean that you were sent away for telling the truth?" Vasthai asked Phoenix while giving her undivided attention. Phoenix closed her eyes as if she was going to a place in her mind that she did not want to venture to. Her eyes were closed but she still had tears flooding down her face.

Vasthai leaned over and placed her arm around her and said, "I didn't mean to bring out any emotions that were going to make you upset. You don't have to tell me if you don't want to." Vasthai wanted to make her feel comfortable so that she would spill her guts and confide in her.

Phoenix opened her eyes and looked directly into Vasthai's eyes and said, "No, I need to talk to someone. This situation is the main reason why I have not been around my daughter, parents or brother. It's what drove me to drugs. This situation is why I changed my name. My birth name is

Sandra Michelle Williams. I changed it to Phoenix after Kennedy was two. My family was extremely close. In 1984, when I turned sixteen and my brother was eighteen I was still a virgin, but I had a boyfriend. On March 10, 1984 my brother came into my room in the middle of the night and started to fondle me. I was so afraid to scream...I just let him have his way."

She breathed in deeply and continued her story. "I could feel his dick getting hard and it was touching my thigh. I closed my eyes and imagined that I was somewhere else. When he stuck it inside of me, he covered my mouth to muffle my cries of pain. When he was done, he injected me with his seed. Then he just got up and left my room. Two months later my mother took me to the doctor and they informed me that I was pregnant. When my father came home I had to tell them who the father was. I told them that James had come into my room and my mother told me that I was a liar!!! In April I was sent to stay with my grandmother in Mississippi."

Vasthai could not believe what she was hearing!!! She was just told that two years before she was raped that James, that bastard raped his own sister!!! It all made sense now!!! Kennedy wanted in on getting revenge on her father/uncle.

When Phoenix finished telling her deep, dark secret Vasthai began to wonder if Kennedy already knew about her rape? Why did she act as if she had not already known when they first met?

"Phoenix...I am truly sorry you had to endure something as cruel as what your own flesh

and blood did to you. What happened was not your fault. Did he know that you were pregnant and what did your parents do to him for violating you?" Vasthai asked her. She just had to know.

Phoenix was glad to be getting some off her baggage off her chest. She had to confess it all. "My parents and I kept the pregnancy a secret. They never even confronted him about what they both knew was true!!! They made me feel as if I invited this to happen!!! I was the one sent away, but when I found out that he had gotten into trouble for the same thing two years later our parents sent him to Mississippi, too. From what I understood there was a bounty on his head and he had to get out of the city. When Nana told me that James was coming there, I knew, I could never again in life be in the same room with him. I called my father's mother and Kennedy and I took the bus to Milwaukee. We stayed there until my granny passed away." Phoenix said.

After taking a pause she continued her confessional. "I was young and had no idea how to be a mother, especially to a child that was fathered by my brother. I did the best that I could do with the help of my grandmother, but when I started using, I neglected my child. Kennedy overheard my mother and me arguing one day when she decided to come and visit. My mother only came to see about us every now and again, but she would send money for Kennedy through my granny. This particular visit was in 1996 when I was twenty-eight and Kennedy was twelve. She heard us arguing about the drugs and me not taking care of Kennedy. I told her the

reason I was strung out was because of what James had done to me; and it was time she got her head from between her ass and admit the truth…her son was my child's father!! Kennedy walked in the room when she heard what I said and it killed me!!!"

Phoenix looked at Vasthai as she continued to cry her soul clean. She stopped and began again with her story. "That was the last time I saw her before she died. When she passed, I left Kennedy with my granny and focused on dulling my pain with dope. It wasn't until my granny died that I regained custody of her, but I still wasn't clean. Our relationship has been strained. I guess we will have a chance to make it right between us now."

Vasthai and Phoenix both sat the remainder of the flight in silence. Each of them was in their own thoughts.

Vasthai had a newfound hate in her heart after hearing what was told to her. She had to speed this plan up because she was ready to kill this motherfuckin nigga and put his ass out of his misery!!!

Long Time, No Hear
Chapter 18

     Patrick was riding to his office when a number appeared on his cell he hadn't seen in quite a while. It was his frat brother Rodney calling from Mississippi. When they were at Howard University they had both pledged Kappa Alpha Psi. Patrick was the ace and Rodney was his duce. They became brothers during the process of crossing over.

     It was like Rodney had ESP because Patrick was going to call him that week, too. Patrick answered his phone and said, "What's going with you...my nigga!!" He said excitedly into the phone. Rodney was so glad to hear his voice. He needed to talk to someone. He knew Patrick would keep his secrets.

     "Do you have time to talk because I have a lot to get off my chest!!!" Rodney said hoping that his frat would have time to hear him out.

     Patrick pulled to the side of the street. He was ready to hear whatever he had to say because he knew that if he was in need; Rodney would be there for him.

     "Talk to me I am all ears!!" He said. Rodney started the conversation off slowly before he got to the meat of what he needed to say. "There has been a lot going down here in the 'sip! I got to get out of the city. I need for you to help me secure a job at your hospital. I did some unethical shit!!! I sold out

one of my patients for a nice compensation package. I was approached by a woman named Kennedy and she wanted information on my patient James Williams, the same guy that you keep tabs on. Dog, what have I gotten involved in? What makes this even more fucking strange is the nigga she wanted info on is now being indicted on charges of having sex with a minor!! "

Patrick listened as his mind wandered. Who was this person checking up on James? He needed to get him to where he was so that they could talk face to face.

"What did she want to know and how did she know that he was even one of your patients?" He asked his friend. Rodney had not even taken the time to think about those questions. All he was concerned about was getting his money.

"Look, I don't want to discuss anymore of this over the phone. I will be there tomorrow. I am looking for another house and I hope a new job with your help."

Patrick had a strange feeling come across him. He knew that it was not coincidence that another woman was inquiring about the man who raped his wife.

"Rodney, when you get here stay at my house. The kids would love to spend time with their Uncle Rodney!!! We will talk about this when you get here. Call me with your flight info." Patrick told his lifelong friend.

The two talked for a few more minutes before ending their phone call. He was glad that his boy had come to him with this information. Patrick

wasn't even mad with him about selling one of his patients out. Shit, money talks and the bullshit walks. He was going to do all he could for his friend.

Before he pulled back into the traffic he made a few calls. He called in some favors. Rodney was going to have a new job and new home to view when he arrived in town.

Everything is not Always What it Seems...
Chapter 19

Kennedy walked into the court with her briefcase in hand wearing an all black Armani pinstriped suit. James was denied bond and they were now in court for the setting of his court date. However, there were forces working against her client. Monica had offered a plea deal that was lenient.

It was her job to persuade him to take the deal. Part of the plan was the sooner that James was in jail the faster his demise would befall him. Kennedy had been patient thus, far but now her patience was wearing thin.

"Are all of the parties in the case of state of Mississippi versus James Williams present?" the judge asked. In unison both Kennedy and Monica both replied "yes".

"Let's get these proceedings started. Mr. Williams, do you understand that you are being charged with one count of statutory rape?" The judge asked as he looked directly at him. James inhaled deeply and spoke up so that all who were there could hear him. "Yes, I understand the charges."

"This is a hearing to set a court date for trial. The court date for your trial will be set for July 16th 2009. Are there any objections about this date from either the defense or the prosecution?" The judge asked both of the attorneys that were there in his courtroom.

The hearing was less than twenty minutes and it was over. As James was led away from the courtroom by the bailiff he turned around to see if his wife was there. His eyes were immediately directed to the woman who was sitting next to his wife. He stopped in his tracks and looked at who he thought was a woman from his past...his sister, Sandra.

The two of them locked eyes for what seemed an eternity. He was speechless and the only thing that he could do was shed a tear. His tear was for the one thing that he regretted doing to her. What he had done to others. James mouthed the words, "I'm sorry."

He hung his head in shame and was led back to his cage. For the first time he felt as if he was in purgatory as if he was about to pay for all of the fucked and foul things that he had done to so many in his life.

Kennedy and Monica who were still in the courtroom both saw the exchange between James and Phoenix. Kennedy had the biggest smirk on her face when she saw the man she wanted dead was seeing a ghost. A ghost that he thought he had left in his past. The entire scene worked just as they had wanted.

As the courtroom was emptied of people Kennedy, Monica, Layce and Phoenix went their separate ways. They wanted to keep their connection to each other as incognito as possible. The more that they gave people the impression that they did not know each other the better it would be not to connect them to what the ultimate goal was…murder.

Several hours later Kennedy waited for James to be escorted in the attorney/client room. She had some paperwork for him to sign and a surprise that was going to fuck with his psyche. Kennedy made sure that she had everything she needed, including a television with a DVD player in the room.

James finally walked in the room and had a seat in front of her. She wasted no time getting to the purpose of the meeting.

"James, I know that we just had the hearing for the court date. However, the DA's Office recently presented me with a plea deal for you. The terms of the deal are that you waive your right to a trial by a jury of your peers, you pled guilty to the charge of sexual misconduct with a minor, and you will spend three years in the FCI Yazoo City Medium Security Prison. With good behavior you could be released in eighteen months." She told him while sliding the papers in front of him to sign.

James looked at her with a look of defeat. He had become emotionally drained from all of the many things that were happening to him. He chalked up his situation to karma. With the overwhelming feelings of guilt, regrets, baggage,

and immense sadness James put up no resistance to signing the papers. He was ready to face his fate and spare his family the humiliation of a public trial.

Once James' John Hancock was on the dotted line Kennedy placed the documents neatly in a folder and back into her briefcase. She looked at James and passed him a cigarette. They both began to smoke when the door opened and walked in Layce, Leah, Chris and a mystery woman.

He stood up and rushed over to his wife and daughter and gave them both a hug. When he stepped back to look at them he had the feeling that they were not happy to see him.

"What's up with the faces? Y'all don't look to happy to see me. I have some good news. I will be home in eighteen months!!!" James said.

Layce looked at her husband. She was disgusted just from having to look at him. She was there to be the bearer of good news for her, but devastating news for him.

Chris looked on as his woman was about to tell his boy that he was fucked. He causally pulled out a chair and sat next to the forty-two inch flat screen television.

"James, you need to back up from my woman!!" Chris said throwing salt into his manhood. He wanted him to know that he was now the man in his wife's life.

"Nigga, what the fuck did you say!!! I know you ain't disrespecting me and my wife!! I will break my fucking foot off in your ass nigga!!!" James said as he stood toe to toe with Chris.

Layce saw that it was about to be drama and she quickly defused it. "James, sit down we need to talk!!!" She said as she grabbed his handcuffed hands and led him back to his seat at the table. Once they were both seated she reached inside of her purse and pulled out a manila folder and a DVD.

"What the fuck is going on!!" James' nose was flaring and he was breathing heavily. Layce pulled out the contents that were inside of the envelope and laid them in front of James. His eyes got wide as he looked at the many pictures that showed him with many of his mistresses. He picked up the one that he saw with him and his son.

"Where did you get these from?"He asked. Layce looked at him and she saw no remorse for what he did. No remorse for his betrayal to a woman who had been down for him for so many years.

"Where I got these pictures are not your concern!!! Furthermore, what I do from here on out is not your concern. You, see this meeting between us is a farewell!! These pictures were all the motivation I needed to set your stupid ass up for a crime that you did not commit!!!" She told him.

Kennedy busted out laughing at the comment that was just made and James glared at her with the look of death. She returned his stare with the same intensity.

Layce looked at Kennedy and smiled. James was on the verge of speaking when Layce cut him off and continued what she had to say. "James, you see, I was visited by a woman that you raped many years ago by the name of Vasthai. She

schooled me on the man that I had no idea about. You see the night that I was supposedly raped and you raped your daughter never occurred!!"

James was more confused than ever. He was there and they both knew what the fuck took place in that house. "What the fuck are you talking about Layce?" He said. As he was waiting for a response Chris leaned over and retrieved the DVD that was in Kennedy's extended hand. He placed the movie in the DVD player and pressed "play".

Layce got up from her chair and walked to the television. She pushed the large television directly in front of him because she wanted him to see this up close and personal. She placed her finger on he screen and said, "How well do you know my body James? Apparently, not well at all because as you can see this woman does not have that signature birthmark on the outer side of her thigh!! If you look even closer the woman in the DVD doesn't even have my same facial features, but she does resemble me!!! Now, as we fast forward to the fucking of your daughter, let's examine her as well!" Layce was just getting started!!!

James looked at the woman on the screen and as he looked closer at the woman he saw that she was not his wife, but someone who closely resembled her. The bitch set me up for the downfall!!!

He looked at her and spit in her face. When the spit reached Layce's face she back handed him so hard that he incurred a nose bleed.

James stood up in front of his wife as if he was about to physically assault her. Layce stood her

ground. She had been waiting for this day, the day that her husband realized that she was the cause of him going to prison. As she stood in front of the man she shared a bed with for many years, the man she now shared her bed with came from behind her and stood in front of her.

"What nigga!! What the fuck you think you about to do!!! I will blow your fuckin cranium off if you think what I think you are thinking!!!" Chris said as he placed his hand on his gun that was concealed underneath his shirt.

James knew that he could not handle his business right then. He decided to let it go and figure out how he would get the ones who betrayed him later. As he sat down he locked eyes with his daughter and instantly became angered. "Why the hell are you showing this shit in front of my baby?" he said.

When he mentioned his daughter Layce laughed as if her life depended on it. This was about to be the shocker of his life. She walked over to the mystery woman; the girl whom he was referring to.

Layce, Leah and the mystery woman walked over to the table where James and Kennedy were. Layce looked at her and said, "Sweetie, please tell this man what your name is and what you do for a living."

The girl was paid handsomely for her participation in the infamous sex scandal. The woman who stood before James bore a striking resemblance to his daughter, but she was not a sixteen year old girl she was a twenty-four year old woman who was blessed to still have an innocent

face like a child. In fact, all of the players from that one night were paid porno stars. "My name is Passion. I work in the adult entertainment industry" She told James.

James looked at the girl and could not believe his eyes!!!This had to be his daughter!!! There was no way that she was not. Why would she lie to him? "Leah, you don't have to lie to me!! I know my child." He was cut off by the sounds of the DVD resuming play. All eyes were directed at the porno show before them.

Layce zoomed in on Passion in the video and zoomed in on a tattoo that she had on her hand. The tattoo on her hand distinctly showed the name Carlos. When he saw the tattoo and the word Carlos, James knew then that he was set up!!!

Leah looked at her father and said, "I'm sorry daddy... I had to go along with the plan." She could not stand to look at her father any longer and she ran out the room crying her eyes out. James watched his daughter leave and his heart broke.

The most sickening thing was that his wife helped with the set up. He could get over her fucking his boy because to him you never fought over pussy.

Kennedy was thoroughly enjoying the episode that was happening in front her. She would have paid money to see this shit on pay-per-view!!!

Kennedy looked at her client and said, "Well, it looks like you are fucked!!! You should be careful what you do to others. This is only the beginning for you!!! As you can see... the three people you thought would not betray you did. Your

wife, your attorney, and your friend fucked you!!! We each have our own motives for wanting to do you in!!! Oh you just sleep on this and wonder when the next round is coming!!!" Kennedy said.

James stood up and looked at Kennedy and said, "What the fuck…you in on this shit too!!!? How the fuck you going to sit here and hear that a crime was never committed and do nothing to get me out of this predicament!!!?"

Kennedy looked at him and with a smile on her face said, "James, I provided you with an adequate defense. Furthermore, our business is done!!!"

Kennedy gathered her things and headed for the door. When she left the room, a few minutes later Layce, Chris, and Passion left right behind her. James was left there by himself with his thoughts.

All he could do was cry. He was going to prison on the account of some bullshit!!!! How could he have not realized that the women in the room were not in fact his wife and daughter? He felt like the best fool!! Then he replayed Kennedy's words again and again in his mind, "*Well, it looks like you are fucked!!! You should be careful what you do to others. This is only the beginning for you!!! As you can see, the three people that you thought would not have betrayed you did…your wife, your attorney, and your friend!!! We each have our own motives for wanting to do you in!!! Oh you just sleep on this and wonder when the next round is coming*"

The door opened and the guard walked in to escort him back to his cell. He had just had a lot

135

placed on his plate. It was too much to digest. He had learned of the betrayal that was initiated by Vasthai.

As he looked back on the last few months he went back to the night that he escorted Tyrone James to see a visitor. He thought back to the woman who was there visiting with him. He played her face back in his mind. She looked familiar, but because the room was dark he could not get a clear look at her. "Could that have been Vasthai?" He said out loud.

As he was reminiscing on the many past events that had occurred, the cell door was opened and the guard said, "Williams, you are being transported to Yazoo City."

James got ready to go to his new home. He was going to have time to think of how to pay each and every one of those bitches back who betrayed him. He was going to be like Tupac when he plotted on his enemies… *"Revenge is like the sweetest joy next to getting pussy"*.

James was now officially known as inmate 152818. He complied with the plea deal and was now on the bus headed to the prison where he once was one of the HNIC's there.

His mind was clouded with thoughts of how he was going to kill everyone who had put him in this predicament. James was in his own world and had not realized that the bus ride had come to an end. He was at his new home.

He was led into the prison and was processed just like the rest of the niggas there with him. James knew the process and went along so he could get along. As he was going through the system he could feel the stares of all of his former co-workers looking at him with piercing eyes.

James kept his head up and met their stares with a stare of his own. In his eyes he showed a man who was bruised but not broken. After he was being processed he headed to his cell.

He was hoping that he would be able to get a cell to himself but he didn't get his hopes up to high because he knew overpopulation was a muthafucka!!

James had his bed sheets and other essentials in his arms as the guard walked side by side with him down the B block corridor. He tuned all of the other inmates out who were talking shit to

him as he looked straight ahead until the guard stopped him at his cell.

James knew the routine and turned and faced his cell. The guard turned and yelled out, "Open cell 30!!!" He waited to be free from the constraint of the metal handcuffs and walked into his new home. He looked at his surroundings and saw that he was sharing the small 6x9 area with someone else.

He stepped inside his cell and placed his meager belongings on the empty bed. James looked over at the other bed that was directly in front of his and thought, "Who is this nigga I got to room with?" As James was placing his jailhouse sheets on his bed in walked his cell mate.

The two men instinctively gave each other the signature head nod. James finished fixing his bed and sat on the bed. His cellmate sat across from him and said, "What's up!!!? My name is Tyrone. Who are you?"

James stared at the young man who sat across from him. His face looked like a younger version Idris Elba, the actor who played Stringer Bell on The Wire.

He could tell that there was something different about him. It was something about his disposition and energy. "I know you know who I am! I mean my face has been on all of the jailhouse television screens for the last few months!!" James spat at the man who called himself Tyrone.

It was true that Tyrone knew about him. He was fishing to see where this nigga was at mentally. From where Tyrone was sitting, the nigga seemed

as if he was bitter for getting caught on some shit he had done. One thing you could tell was someone who was guilty from someone who was innocent.

"Look, nigga when you were on the outside you were running some shit!!! While you here behind these cell bars nigga, you are nobody but a fucking number!! The next time you get out of pocket with me it will be some fucking furniture movin in this tiny ass cell!!! So I suggest that we start this shit off right cause I don't want no drama!!! We understand one another!!!?" Tyrone told him in a calm but threatening tone.

Although, Tyrone was well liked and respected among the inmates and COs alike...he was known to knock a nigga on his back if needed to.

James looked at his cellmate and decided that what the young boy was telling him was true. He was just another number. He was not in control, the state of Mississippi was. It was a prison thing. Now, the two of them had an unspoken mutual understanding.

It was then that James truly understood where he was. He needed to get his mental shit together if he was going to make it his eighteen months. He couldn't afford for his stay there to be prolonged because he had unfinished business to handle when he returned home.

Information is Power
Chapter 21

Rodney landed at the airport and picked up his luggage. He was glad to be out of Mississippi and although his time there was for the most part good, it was time for him to start somewhere new. His conscious burned because he had taken and broken the oath of doctor/patient confidentiality.

He was walking toward the airport exit when he heard his name being called by a familiar voice. "Rodney...Rodney!!!" He heard the voice of Patrick calling him. Rodney quickly turned to face the sound of the voice and saw Patrick walking toward him. The two of them embraced in a hug and gave each other their Kappa Nupe handshake.

"What's up nigga!!? How you doing!!!?" Rodney said to his closet friend. The two men looked each other over. It had been a while since they had last seen one another.

"Man, I'm living. Just trying to make it!! You know how it is. The same shit, different day!!" Patrick said to him as they both walked towards the parking lot approaching Patrick's BMW.

The two of them walked into Bahama Breeze and were seated at a booth that was off in a secluded corner away from the other customers. The waiter came to the table and they placed their orders.

As they waited for the orders to come to the table Patrick started the conversation. "So tell me what happened. I mean whatever you did I don't give a fuck about that. You know I wouldn't tell anyone about what you are about to tell me." He told him as their drinks were being placed on the table in front of them.

Rodney looked at his friend and thought, *"That was the best thing about Patrick. He was upfront and to the point with his shit. He was never the one for the bullshit. He just said what was on his mind. That was one of the reasons why they were friends."*

Rodney took a sip of his White Russian and let the alcohol run down his throat. He needed to confess his sins to someone and he was glad that he was telling someone that he knew he could trust.

"Man the shit was so funny how it all popped off!! I mean I was just leaving from the office one night and out of nowhere there she was standing at my car. When I got closer and saw her face I was mesmerized by her beauty" Rodney started his story, but stopped when the waiter returned to the table with their food.

The two men ate for a few minutes in silence before Rodney continued his story. "She stepped to me, extended her hand and introduced herself. She said that her name was Kennedy and that she had a business proposition for me. So, I invited her to have dinner with me so we could discuss it in private."

Patrick was listening to every word that he was hearing and taking mental notes. He needed to

know exactly who this chick was. He had a feeling that he was going to have to hire his friend to do some investigation. He had a feeling that Rodney was targeted for a specific reason.

"So what was she talking about when you two were at the restaurant?" Patrick asked. Rodney took another bite of his ribs and wiped his hand on the napkin and said, "She asked me to give her some information on a patient of mine. At first I told her hell no!!! I mean… I was not about to lose my job, reputation and license to practice to help this bitch!!! Then she wrote on her napkin a note to me and left her business card. After that, she left. I read the note and it said, *"I will pay you $500k for your services."*

"I mean when I saw that, I was thinking hard about it then. I looked at her business card and was shocked because she is one of the best defense lawyers in the area. Kennedy is so good that all of the dope boys retain her. She charges them out the muthafuckin ass because she always finds a way to get them off."

The two of the men finished their meals and talked about other things. Rodney wanted to finish the conversation in the privacy of the car.

"Man, I got you!!! All you have to do is interview for the position and the job is basically yours. The interview is just a formality. Not only that, I called my realtor friend and she has a few houses that she wants you to look at." Patrick told Rodney. After hearing those words Patrick's face lit up. He was so happy to hear those words coming from his boy's mouth. He knew Patrick would look

out, but, damn he didn't know the shit would be that quick.

Within the last three weeks Rodney had been able to sell his home, close all of his bank accounts, and resign from his position at the prison.

He was a valuable asset to the prison as he was the psychiatrist for all of the prison inmates and employees. He also had a thriving private practice that he sold to his assistant psychiatrist for one dollar. The only thing that he wanted to do was pack his shit and leave.

The last time he met with Kennedy he had a bad feeling...as if there was something boiling underneath the surface. He was already in to deep and he needed to cut his ties before he was ruined completely. When he left Mississippi he left without even a mumble of goodbye to anyone.

Patrick drove back to his home. He and Rodney had spent the rest of the day looking at houses. Rodney had finally settled on one that he fell in love with. He put an offer in on it. Patrick told him to stay at his house until the contract was finalized.

"Uncle Rodney!! What are you doing here!!!?" Kamron and Tyson said as they both ran to their uncle and gave him big hugs.

After they spent time with the kids Patrick and Rodney retreated to the entertainment room. Patrick turned on the 50 inch flat screen. After the television was tuned into ESPN he went to the bar and poured them drinks. As Patrick was fixing the beverages, Rodney left to retrieve James' file from his briefcase.

They were both chilling when Rodney looked at his friend and said, "Let me finish telling you my plight. A few days had passed and I had not given my encounter with Kennedy anymore thought when she showed up at my practice. I didn't want to cause a seen so I invited her into my office. She sat at my desk and I knew what she came there for. I told her if she wanted my help that she needed to provide half of the money up front and in cash. She told me that she would be back with half of the money next week and she wanted to receive half of the file in return. I never asked her what she wanted the file for, but some time later the same nigga whose file that she requested got arrested for having sex with a minor."

Patrick was tripping on what he had just heard. James was locked up for fucking a minor. "What do you mean that he got popped for sexing a minor? Is he locked up now? What happened???" Patrick asked.

Rodney told his old friend everything from the DVD that was on the news, to Kennedy coming back to him to ask him about a prior rape that James had confessed to in one of his sessions.

After the two of them talked Rodney let Patrick read the original file. Patrick read the entire file in the comfort of his bedroom.

Patrick took an extended leave of absence from the hospital and asked his father-in-law to watch Kamron and Tyson. He gassed up his Beamer with only a bag in the back seat and was headed to Mississippi.

Patrick read James' psych file that he obtained from Rodney; and he knew in his heart that Vasthai was in the city plotting revenge on that nigga.

Before he left home he did some investigating. He Google the arrest record to see the charges that were brought against James. When he saw both Monica and Kennedy's pictures in one of the articles that he was reading he got a nauseated feeling in the pit of his stomach.

The picture of Monica and Kennedy looked familiar because he had seen their pictures before!!! They were with the other pictures that his wife had in her box that was at her father's house. Patrick was glad that he had made a duplicate of everything that was hidden in Vasthai's secret box.

Locked UP...Adjusting to Prison
Chapter 22

James had been Mississippi state property for three months. He now understood how men acted like heathens. They were confined to an overpopulated space where there was no effort to reform the minds of the imprisoned.

The adjustment for James was quick. He learned to keep to himself and only associate with his cellmate, Tyrone. All that he was concerned about was doing his time. He and Tyrone had become tight in the ninety days they had known each other.

Whenever he talked with the Tyrone he felt an overwhelming connection to him, as if he had known him from a previous life. Their souls were now intertwined in the present life. They never discussed the outside world because the outside was dead to those inside the prison walls.

They always talked about the similarities between the crimes in which they were convicted and the many regrets that they had in their lives.

Never once did the either one of them mention names of their loved ones. Each day passed slower than the next, but they took it in stride and pressed forward.

"Williams you have mail!" the CO shouted as he passed by the cell and handed him the letters that were addressed to him. James retrieved the letters that he was not expecting and sat on the bed to read them. He was surprised to get a letter from his wife and one from his mistress that he had his son with.

"What the fuck does this bitch want!!!? Ain't shit we need to discuss!!!" James said as he opened Layce's letter. His eyes began to read the letter:

James,
I know you think we don't have anything to discuss, but there is one thing that we need to get resolved. Place my name on your visitor's list and I will be there next week so we can talk.
Layce

James was tripping on what he just read, but his curiosity was piqued. He actually wanted to hear what she had to say. He opened the second letter and smiled when Destiny wanted to see him and bring their son, too. James began to think about starting his life over with Destiny.

Out of all of the women that he fucked around on Layce with; she was the only one who was down for him and was willing to stick by him no matter what. Once upon a time he believed that he had found those same qualities in Layce, but now he knew better.

Layce was a good girl that had gone bad. As he reminisced about his wife he began to blame himself for how she turned out. He would have

continued to have had that happy home if only he could have controlled his dick! Now his wife was getting dick from the dude who was supposed to be cool with him.

As he thought about the pending visit of both Layce and Destiny his dick got hard and he found his hand reaching to relieve that nut that had been building up inside of him. He jacked his dick until his cum spattered all over his hand.

He washed up the semen and his hands and headed out of his cell to the outside where Tyrone was. As he was walking to the weight area...He had the thought of just letting the shit go.

He felt that the revenge that he had in his heart was his retribution for all of the shit that he had done. Little did he know as he was releasing his anger, there were others who were getting ready to exact their revenge on him.

Getting the Ducks in a Row....
Chapter 23

Vasthai wanted to wait for the James to get acclimated to his new surroundings before she rallied the troops to enact part two of the plan. Part of the deal she had with her alliance was that the last payment of the money was to be dispersed only when they finished what they agreed to do and when they vanished without a trace, into the night.

She had sent out texts via the burners to everyone saying, *"Its time for everyone to get ready. Make your money and dip!!! Your directions for step two of the plan will be sent to you via courier service."*

Vasthai sat on her bed and pulled out her box. She looked at the pictures that she had there. She looked over each one of them intently. There was one picture that she held up and placed to her chest. She was waiting for everything to be over so that she could get on with her life and start fresh with the person in the picture.

After looking over everything that was in the box she pulled out each person's individual instructions, placed them inside of an Express Courier envelope and sealed them. She called the courier service for delivery.

Vasthai finished getting dressed for the day and headed out of the door. She wanted to meet with Kennedy, Monica and Layce. She sent out a text to them and told them to meet her at the Starbucks at 7pm.

She needed to make sure that they were still down for the cause. Vasthai went to an Olive Garden and was just being seated when she saw Chris. He was there with some of his co-workers for lunch, while Vasthai was there to pass the time until the meeting.

Chris excused himself from the table and walked over to where Vasthai was sitting. "Join me!" Vasthai said, as she lifted her wine glass to him; inviting him to sit so they could have a conversation.

Chris pulled out the empty chair from the other side of the table and sat down. He was intrigued by her. From what he understood from talking with Layce she was the mastermind behind James' debacle. He wanted to pick her mind. He wanted to know what her motivation for having hate in her heart so deep that she wanted to do that nigga in.

"What's up with you!!?" He asked her as he folded his arms across his chest. Vasthai looked at the man who was sitting across from her. She knew that she needed to keep her cool because he was an important part of her plan.

"Nothing. I am just here passing the time. I have an appointment in a few hours." She responded as she placed salad in her mouth.

Chris looked at her and he got the feeling that she was trying to be cordial, however, the tone in her words gave him the distinct impression that she was hiding a deep rooted hate for him as well.

"What's up with the attitude in your voice!!!? I thought that we were cool, Vasthai?" He stated.

Vasthai knew where he was going with this conversation and she needed to turn it around. "I apologize if I came off rude. I have a lot on my mind. You do understand William don't you?" She said as she waited for his reaction.

Chris knew that he misheard what she called him. He had not been called William, since he and James were both shipped to Mississippi. "Who did you just call me?" He asked.

"I called you Chris. What did you think I called you? I'm sorry I don't understand what you are talking about." Right on cue, her cell phone rang and she picked it up and placed the receiver to her ear.

"If you don't mind I need to take this call in private." Vasthai said, as she waited for him to leave the table.

Chris got up from his chair and headed to the table where his co-workers were. As he was walking back to the table he had a bad feeling in the pit of his stomach.

He felt as if he had been found out!!! Long ago, he did some foul shit. Everyday since that time he regretted his actions and tried to repent for his sins by trying to live his life right. As result of

trying to change his life he changed his face through plastic surgery and assumed a new identity.

When he came back to Mississippi to take the job as a CO at the prison in Jackson, not in his wildest dream would he have thought he was going to see an old friend…his friend James!

Although, James did not recognize him at first, he soon realized that it was his friend William from back home, now going by the name of "Chris".

The two of them became close again until he realized that he was dogging his wife out with every pussy-hole that he could find. He tried to push up on Layce, but she was not trying to give him any play.

When the shit popped off with the arrest of James he was right there to fill the void. Now that he had her he was ready to get this shit over with so that they could be a family.

Vasthai watched as Chris left with his group of friends. She knew that he was thinking "how did she know his real government name that his momma gave him." What he didn't know was that she had been planning this shit for so long that she made sure that all of her information was accurate and on point.

She did her homework well because once it was all said and done she was killing the men who raped her and her son was coming home.

Chris didn't know that she knew that he was the other man there the night she was raped. He was the one who assaulted her too!!! It didn't matter to her one little bit that he was truly sorry for what he

did or that he was trying to make amends by being good to every woman that he was in a relationship with. This made no difference to Vasthai, he had to pay too.

Vasthai set it up so that Chris and James would be working together at the same prison; the same prison where her son was. She also knew that Chris wanted Layce and she saw her opening to get them together after James was arrested. The purpose of getting them together was so that he would have his guard down.

Although, Vasthai had a little bit of work done to her face over the years she still thought she looked the same as she did when she was sixteen.

She could understand why James and Chris did not recognize her...but that was all good. She ate the rest of her lunch and was waiting on 7pm to roll around.

The Meeting

Vasthai was pulling into the Starbucks parking lot when she saw that Monica, Layce, and Kennedy were already sitting at one of the tables on the patio.

Monica and Layce were at least acting civil to each other in public. Vasthai knew better. If the circumstances were different they would have been going blow for blow like Holyfield and Tyson.

She stepped out of the car and went inside to order a tall Caramel Macchiato. Vasthai was going to need something to keep her alert while she held this meeting. As she approached the awaiting women she could sense their impatience.

Vasthai strolled over to her clique of soldiers wearing her Coach shades, hiding her eyes from them. She had no intentions of letting them see her thoughts through her eyes.

"Good evening ladies!!! How are we all doing tonight!!?" She said to them as she took her seat at the table amongst them. They acknowledged her with cordial hellos.

"Ladies, I have asked you here tonight because it is time for this to go down. As you all know I picked each of you for my own personal reasons and each of you have chosen to take part in my plan for your own reasons, as well. Let's just keep it 100 with each other!!!! I know why each and every one of you want James gone, even those who think that I don't know." Vasthai said directing her stare at Kennedy.

Kennedy knew Vasthai's comment was directed at her. Kennedy was sure she was just bluffing and she was not going to give her the satisfaction of telling Vasthai her true motivation.

Although, she was sure that Vasthai had no idea about her conception she needed to throw a rock in the crowd to see if she would get hit or throw the rock back.

"If you think you know about our motives; why don't you share them with the rest of us!!!? Kennedy said.

Vasthai was glad to see that her comment had not gone unnoticed. It was time for her to tell and ensure that all of them were going to do their part.

"Let me start with Layce and I will come to you last Kennedy. Layce you agreed because your husband has another family with your friend and because, I know that you are the cause of your friend's child being sick. Monica, James raped you. Also, I know that you got your promotion to be the District Attorney because you fucked the judge. Kennedy, you see, I know who your father/uncle is. Your mother had you from the seed of her brother James."

When Vasthai said that last bombshell Layce and Monica both looked at Kennedy with a look of shock and disbelief in their eyes. Not only had all of their secrets been revealed, but she was living proof of all of what Vasthai said.

Vasthai reached into her purse and pulled out three envelopes each addressed to each of them individually. She handed them to each of them and waited for them to look inside. As each woman opened the envelope they all looked around the table. They had just opened the proof of their secrets.

"Before, you say one word Kennedy, Let me say this, I too was raped by James and got pregnant from him. He has a son that he knows nothing about. I know what it is like to have hate so deep in your soul that the only way that you can cure that hurt is by eradicating it. I know about feeling as if you did something wrong and foul. You can't blame yourself for how you came into this world, but you can inflict that pain on the one who gave it to you in the first place." Vasthai sincerely said to her.

Kennedy could feel the tears forming in her eyes, but she refused to let them see her cry. Her plan was for no one to know about James being her father/uncle until it was time to do him in, but her plan backfired on her.

She was at a lost for words! She could not articulate the words to express how she was feeling. The extreme feelings of guilt, shame and self-loathing overwhelmed Kennedy.

"Ladies, I will never use any of this information against you. I just want to let you know that I know the truth about why you are working with me. Now, your individual directions should be to you by tomorrow morning. In the meantime it is time for Kennedy and Monica to put in your two week notice at work. Layce the sale of your house should be complete by the end of this week. Make sure that you leave no forwarding information and you bring along with you only the people that you want to start your new life with. Once this deed is done we all will be like ghosts in the night. When everything is done money will be waiting for you in your offshore accounts." Vasthai told them as she handed them all their respective piece of paper with their offshore account numbers on them.

"Oh and before I forget…Layce make sure that you make your daughter the beneficiary of James' life insurance and make sure that you specify that in the case of his death that you want the money placed in a trust for her. That way there would be no investigation of you." Vasthai told her as she rose from her chair.

Vasthai was preparing to leave the women when Monica said, "Vasthai, once this is over will you be satisfied?"

Vasthai looked at Monica and pulled her shades off so that she could see her eyes. "Let me tell you all this. When this is over I will be more than satisfied. I will be able to be mended from the bruises that were inflicted on me when I was sixteen. If James could have just kept his dick in his fucking pants; I would have been whole to gave whoever I wanted my pussy!!! When this comes full circle with James gone I will be satisfied!!!" She responded as she headed back to her car.

Vasthai had less then two weeks to go. She was anxious. Layce was going to see James in three days.... It was about to be on!!!

Incognito
Chapter 24

Three months had past since James had gone to prison. Little did James know his purgatory was about to heat up. Vasthai was at her home away from home, the Marriott Hotel, when she got a knock at the door. She had not been expecting anybody and was taken by surprise when she heard the knocking.

She looked through the door's peephole and saw her husband standing on the other side of the door. *"Shit! What the fuck is he doing here!?"* She thought to herself. Patrick was growing impatient as he waited for the door to open for him. He knew his wife so well that he knew she was thinking, "What he was doing there?"

"Girl, don't make me get ghetto out here!!! Open this fucking door Vasthai!!!" He said through clenched teeth. After she heard those words she opened the door for her husband.

She stepped to the side and let him pass by to get inside the room. "Baby, what are you doing here?! I told you that I was coming home this week sometime." She said as she walked behind him and sat on the bed.

Patrick looked at his wife. He had not seen her in almost three months since she went on this trip to see their son. He was turned on just by the

sight of her beauty and he wanted to be inside of her.

After he felt her pussy walls wrapped around his dick, then he would get to the bottom of why she was really there. He took off his shirt and tossed it on the floor.

Patrick took in Vasthai's beauty before he devoured her with his sexual organ that was pounding, waiting to feel her warm juices escaping her body. He walked over to his wife and without acknowledging her last statement he got on his knees and spread her legs eagle. His hands pulled down her pants and let them hit the floor.

They were both quiet because they both knew what was about to go down. Vasthai missed Patrick and was waiting for him to invade her garden. She closed her eyes and became instantly stimulated from the touch of her husband's hands on her body.

Patrick pushed Vasthai on the bed and his head was planted in her pussy. The taste from her pussy made him rock hard. His dick was so hard he thought he was about to explode before he could feel the warmth of her insides gripping him. He began to flicker his tongue on her clit and Vasthai moaned from the heat.

He continued to lick and suck her pussy until she was moving his head deeper and deeper inside of her. Vasthai arched her back and welcomed his tongue with the juices of her cum. She missed her husband and was glad to have him enter her.

When Patrick felt the juices from her pussy touch his tongue he let them flow down his face. He took his shirt and wiped the pussy juices from his mouth. He took off the rest of his clothes and stood over Vasthai's body.

He admired her body and thought to himself that even after all these years of marriage and the birth of three children his wife's body was still perfect to him. Patrick stroked his dick and could fill the veins pulsate in his hand. He climbed on top of her and entered her as if it was the first time that they were making love.

He let his manhood feel her pussy. He could feel the anticipation from his foreplay was making Vasthai's clit pulsate. Patrick saw that her clit had swollen and was pointing to the heavens above.

He placed his thumb on her clit and began to massage it in circular motions. As he massaged her he began to pump his dick inside of her causing her to orgasm, again.

He pumped his eight inches of love further inside of her. Patrick made sure that he showed his wife how much he missed her. He lifted her legs and pulled her body further down on his dick. When he pulled her body towards his dick Vasthai screamed out in pleasure. As their bodies became one; they both began to throw it to each other.

Patrick turned Vasthai over and pulled her to her knees. He slapped and kissed her ass as he put his dick inside of her from the back. Patrick was pounding her and she was playing with her clit. All that could be heard throughout the room was the sound of their private parts hitting each other;

coupled with the sounds of pleasurable moans.

They found their rhythm and rocked to it. As their bodies became completely drenched in sweat they both came at the same time.

They were both so tired from their sexual episode that they just laid beside each other savoring the mood. Before long they had fallen asleep in the king-sized bed.

It was one in the morning when Patrick heard the sound of water coming from the bathroom. He gathered his bearings and got up from the bed and walked to the bathroom.

When he walked in he saw the steam coming from the shower and decided to join his wife. Vasthai turned around when she felt the shower curtain open. She looked at him with the look of love and seduction all in one.

"Hey baby!" She said to him as she kissed him. The two of them washed each other and fucked in the shower before exiting.

"Come and sit by me Vasthai. We need to talk." Patrick said as he patted the spot next to him on the bed. Vasthai was waiting for him to say those words. She knew he was there for a reason and now she was about to find out what his reasons were. She walked over to the bed and sat next to him.

Patrick ran his fingers through her thick hair and admired her beauty before he started the conversation. "I know about your box with the pictures in it. Vasthai I need for you to tell me the truth. What the fuck have you put into motion? You know I got your back. I am riding with you till

death do us part!!! Let me help you with whatever you are doing. If we work together we can do this shit right and get the hell on with our lives!!! If you can't trust your HUSBAND then who can you trust?!!" He told her as looked her deep in her eyes.

He had been with her since she was sixteen and married to her since she was eighteen. He knew when his wife was telling him the truth and when she was lying.

When Vasthai heard Patrick say he knew about her "secret box" she knew that he knew more than what he was telling her. She knew that she could not lie to him.

She loved her husband and he never would do anything that would jeopardize her marriage or the life that they had together.

She decided to tell him everything. Vasthai and Patrick talked for the next few hours as she explained to him in detail what was going on. He listened intently and took meticulous mental notes as she spoke. When it was all said and done Patrick knew everything.

"If you want this thing to continue to go smoothly you can't go to the jail to visit Tyrone when Layce goes to see James. If he sees you there the nigga might think something is up. Let me go in your place. You lay low until its time to set the shit off right." Patrick said to Vasthai.

Although, Vasthai had planned everything she never took into consideration the element of surprise. Patrick was right. If James saw both his wife and her at the same time visiting he would

think something. He had no idea who Patrick was. It was a perfect solution.

Vasthai called the crew together for one last meeting and explained that Patrick was going to be taking her place when it was time to visit the jail.

After the meeting it was all settled. Now, all Vasthai could do was wait until it was time to meet James one last time before she gave him the business.

And the Truth Shall Set You Free...
Chapter 25

Layce and Patrick were both in the inmate visitor line getting asked a101 questions by the CO. To the unassuming eye they looked like normal visitors going to visit their locked up loved ones, not two people in cahoots with each other. That was what they wanted... to be unsuspecting.

After being processed and made to feel as if they were criminals themselves the two of them waited until they heard James and Tyrone's names being called.

It was about twenty minutes before visiting hours. As the two of them waited, they texted each other back and forth going over the last details on their burner cells.

Tyrone was in his cell doing his daily workout routine when the CO came and said, "Tyrone, you have a visitor!!" He was not expecting to hear that he had a visitor. He thought that it was his mom coming to see him again.

Tyrone nodded his head and turned around to be handcuffed and led to the visiting room. As he was being led to the visitors section he had a lot of thoughts running through his mind.

He had many questions to ask his mom about his biological father, but knew that he had to

do that another time. They had finally reached the location of the prison where the inmates waited for their names to be called so that they could have their visit.

Tyrone looked down the line of his fellow inmates and saw his cellmate James. They had become cool over the last three months. The two of them saw each other and gave a head nod of acknowledgement.

As Tyrone waited to be called his mind went back to the brutal rape that had happened to him when first arrived in the prison.

He didn't know why that shit popped into his head. Tyrone had never had something so violating happen to him before in his life prior to that incident.

Although, he felt that being booty- fucked was his revenge for what he done to Shawn, he was determined to make the niggas pay for taking his asshole! He was in the process of getting at them, but he didn't know was that he would not have a chance to exact his plan because he was about to be amongst the free on the other side of the jail bars.

Just as soon as Tyrone was seated his name was called and he was led to the thick dividing glass that separated prisoner from the free.

When he sat down his whole face lit up like a child on Christmas day because he saw his father sitting in the chair in front of him. Before he sat down and picked up the phone that was placed on the wall for conversing between inmate and visitor the CO un-handcuffed him and walked down the row and did the rest of the inmates.

Tyrone was sitting at the very end of the inmate side of the visiting section. He had not seen James until he was the last one standing waiting for his hands to be free of the hand restraints. Patrick was glad to see his son and wanted to place his arms around him and embrace him.

Patrick picked up the phone and so did Tyrone. Patrick knew he did not have that much time and he needed to get the show on the road. As he looked down the aisle he saw that Layce was playing her part.

"Hey... there son!!! I am so glad to see you!! I know that you were expecting to see your mom but I just came into town and told her that I wanted to see you for myself." Patrick told his son.

It was true that Tyrone was not his by blood, but he loved him just as if he was his and would kill or die for him just as he would for the two that were biologically his.

"What's up pops!! I am glad to see you!! I got that book and the money that you sent me. I was going to write you and tell thank you, but you are here so I am thanking you in person." Tyrone said. As Tyrone and Patrick were talking so were James and Layce.

Layce looked at her husband through the glass and could tell in his eyes that he had forgiven her but he would never again fuck with her.

"What's up Layce? I mean I got your letter so what is the deal? It ain't too much for us to discuss if it ain't about our daughter." He said to her as he was trying to figure out what angle she was coming from.

Just as Layce was feeling sorry for her husband, her feelings of guilt suddenly evaporated when he opened his mouth.

"The only thing that you can do for me nigga is sign these divorce papers!! I just wanted to tell your punk bitch ass to your face that it was over!!" She said. As the two of them were going at it with their heated conversation; Layce saw from the corner of her eye another inmate approaching James from behind.

Before James knew what hit him he was hit square in the face with a combination of blows. Tyrone unmercifully beat James as if he had stolen something from him.

All Tyrone could see in his vision was James, his father raping his mother and how he ended up doing the same fucking thing to his girlfriend.

Several minutes prior to Tyrone commencing to beat James' ass his father had informed him of whom his biological father was. Patrick showed him the picture of his cellmate and he immediately went to retaliate. Tyrone was on James so quickly that he had no chance of defending himself against the assault.

The CO let the beat down go on for three minutes before they stepped in and pulled Tyrone off of his father. After enduring a full three minutes of a vicious beating James' face was fucked up!!!!

His ribs and abdomen were severely cracked and bruised from the repeated stomps from Tyrone's size 10 ½ shoe coming down on him.

Patrick and Layce looked at each other as the other visitors were looking on at the frenzy, in horror. As the other people were watching the fight and being nosy; Patrick and Layce walked past everyone else and headed toward the exit. When they reached the parking lot they both got into their cars and pulled out of the prison facilities.

After the fight was finally broken up and all of the inmates were escorted back to their "homes"; James was rushed to the hospital and Tyrone was sent to the hole for giving the ass whooping.

When Tyrone was left alone in the hole he began to hit the walls with his hands in an effort to calm himself. He could not believe what his father had told him. His words kept replaying in his mind

"Your mother told me that she told you about your real father. When your mother and I were married, I accepted you as if you were my own. To this day you are still my baby. My son, I would lay down my life for yours; just as I would for your sister and brother. The time has come for you to know who your biological father is. I wanted to tell you myself who he is. Your father is James Williams. I have a picture of him if you would like to see how he looks."

When his father showed him the picture of the man who he had been sharing his cell with; all that came to his head was to kill him.

"I can't believe this shit!!! The nigga who raped my mother, my father has been in my face all this time and I had no fucking clue!!! What the fuck!!!" Tyrone said out loud to the four concrete walls that surrounded him. As he was alone with

only his thoughts Tyrone saw visions of killing the man who he just found out was his father.

He was going to kill him for raping his mother and making him just like him… a rapist.

James was in and out of consciousness. The pain medicine he was on had him unaware of his surroundings. As he was going in and out of sleep he saw visions of his attack. He was so deep into his argument with Layce that he had not seen the dude walk up on him.

The attack was so quick that he barely had a chance to defend himself. James was not able to see his attacker but as he drifted off into one of his coma- like sleeps his mind showed him his attacker.

The visions were so vivid. The face of the one who decided to hurt him was none other than the young boy that he had grown to be cool with since his arrival at prison. He was the one that he shared some of his secrets with, the only one who he felt some kind of special bond with…his cellmate Tyrone.

When James saw the image of Tyrone in his mind he tried to wake himself from the dream he was having. The more he tried to open his eyes the worst his beating became in the dream. Just as he felt himself coming into conscience he heard voices in the room.

James could hear but couldn't bring himself to wake from the nightmare that he was having. As he veered between his dream and the voices… he was able to hear the voices say, *"Mr. Williams, sustained damage to his ribs and chest area. He will have to be in the hospital for at least seven to ten*

days before he will be released from the hospital back to the custody of the state." Then he heard the clicking of high heel shoes leave the room and the voice trailed off into the distance.

Several hours later James woke to see that he was alone in his hospital room. As he tried to move his arm he realized that his arm was chained to the bed. He looked toward the door and saw that there was a CO sitting in a chair in front of the door.

He began to feel the pain shoot through his rib and chest area. James was able to locate the nurse call button and press it for help.

When the nurse came in he did not have to say a word. She knew automatically what he wanted. The nurse pulled out the needle from inside of her uniform and inserted the needle into the IV dispensing the pain medicine instantly into his body.

James started to feel the pain in his chest leave him quickly. As he began to close his eyes he drifted off into oblivion…he thought to himself, *"I swear on everything I love that I coming for all of you bitches!!!"*

As he felt his body relax, he nodded off to sleep. He had no idea that he was not going to be around much longer to even get his revenge. His days of living were numbered.

As I have observed, those who plow
evil
and those who sow trouble
reap it.
At the breath of God they are
destroyed;
at the blast of his anger they
perish.
The lions may roar and growl,
yet the teeth of the great
lions are broken.
The lion perishes for lack of prey,
and the cubs of the lioness
are scattered...
JOB 4:8-11

Chapter 26

Vasthai and Patrick checked out of the hotel and walked to the car. They rode in silence as what was about to transpire became apparent. The past week had been a waiting game.

As planned Layce sold her house emptied the bank accounts and was laying low in the cut.

Kennedy and Monica both resigned from their positions leaving without saying goodbye to anyone. Phoenix was just leaving the drug rehab facility, clean for thirty days.

As instructed they left their lives as they knew it and Mississippi behind, to pursue new lives. Once they helped in completing Vasthai's plan against James they would all have $1 million dollars in an offshore account. So it was in everyone's financial best interest to comply with the plan.

It was three in the morning when Vasthai, Patrick, Monica, Kennedy, Layce and Phoenix boarded the prison bus wearing their prison uniforms. As Chris drove the bus to the prison they rode in silent anticipation.

Vasthai and her crew were riding on the bus as Tyrone was getting out of solitary confinement, and James was being wheeled to the front of the hospital waiting for the prison bus to pick him up.

Tyrone was still serving out his punishment in the hole for fucking his father up when the barricaded door swung open. The CO stepped in and handcuffed him. As Tyrone and the guard walked down the corridor, Tyrone realized that he was not going back to his cell when they bypassed the door that led back to his block.

"Yo!!! Where are you taking me?!!" Tyrone asked. The CO continued without answering him. They finally came to the transfer section of the jail. As the CO was filling out the paperwork he looked at the inmate and said, "You are getting a transfer. The bus should be here for you shortly." Tyrone

didn't say anything he sat in the chair and waited for his ride.

The bus pulled up to the hospital where James and the CO who had been assigned to him were. When the bus pulled up the CO helped him get on the bus and made sure that he was seated before exiting. When James got on the bus he saw that there were a lot of people being transported.

He thought that it was odd because when he worked as a CO there were never that many people on the bus at any given time.

The darkness from the night and the darkness from the bus made it hard for him to see any of the other inmates' faces. From where he sat he could see that everything was on the up and up because they were handcuffed and had on their prison uniforms. James wasn't concerned with the rest of them. His eye was on the prize. The prize was named Tyrone.

It took everything within Vasthai and the rest of her accomplices to stay silent. But when no one said anything they realized that it was time to remain calm and let the shit fall where it may. The bus ride was continued in silence as they arrived at the pick up gate to retrieve Tyrone.

Tyrone got onto the bus never once looking at the other people. He found an empty seat and sat down. He was ready to see where his new home was so he could lay down on the hard mattress that he called a bed.

The bus pulled off from the jail and when James saw the bus leaving, and he had not gotten off he knew some shit was not right. He knew that if

he screamed from the back of the bus the driver was not going to hear him; so he decided to wait until the bus stopped at a red light to voice his concern.

What he failed to realize was that that there was not going to be any red lights to stop at... he was headed to his final destination.

Chris drove the bus forty-five miles going South on Highway 49 until he took the exit saying the Natchez Trace Parkway. The ride to their location was no more than an hours' drive and James had fallen asleep among his enemies.

When the bus came to a halt James had the feeling that someone was standing over his body. When his eyes opened he saw the faces of all of the people who had caused his downfall.

Before he was aware of what was going on Chris pulled him by his feet and dragged him down the aisle of the bus. As he was being dragged he could feel the pain coming from his abdomen and ribcage.

When they reached the bus doors, James was made to stand and face his worst fear.... the ones that he had done the most damage to.

"What the fuck!!!! So you punk bitches couldn't face me one on one, but you had to see me all together!! Man, fuck each and every one of you!!" He said with as much malice in his voice as it was in his heart.

James now understood why there were so many people on the bus. He came to the conclusion that he was about to meet his destiny with either heaven or hell. No one said a word they allowed him to vent his peace. Vasthai stepped from the

shadows of the night's darkness and pointed her pink and black 9mm Glock in his face.

She was now face to face with her rapist, her son's father, and the one person who had taken what was not rightfully his when she was sixteen.

"You bitch nigga!!! You want to talk big shit. Don't think I don't have something in store for your ass." She said to him as the most sinister smile crossed her lips.

As Chris was about to move James closer to the Ross R. Barnett Reservoir the woman who he had planned to marry and make his wife stood before him holding a Glock to his temple.

"Layce, what are you doing? What the fuck is going on?!!!" He said. Vasthai never looking at him said, "You see, DNA is a motherfucker!!! Oh when the two of you raped me, the semen from your dick was preserved!!! When you fucked Layce I had the semen compared to my rape kit!!! You see, I figured out that you were the one who was sent to Mississippi with your bitch made friend!! Don't think that the plastic surgery helped you because before I blanked out I remember seeing a glimpse of your face!!!"

Chris was speechless. He thought he had put that part of his life behind him. He was doing the right thing and was now ready to make Layce his wifey. Layce grabbed Chris' gun and gave it to Tyrone since they were unaware that they were going to need another gun for him.

As the moon shone its ray of light on the earth there were six individuals circled around James and Chris with their guns pointed at them.

The games were now starting. Vasthai looked at them and laughed. She looked at everyone else and could tell from the look in their eyes that they were enjoying it, too.

"We are about to play a game of Simon Says. Here are the rules. We are going to go around the circle and tell you what we want you to do. If you do not comply with the requested command you will be shot by the person who asked you to perform the command. Are we clear on these rules!!!? I am going to start first. Simon Says take off your clothes" Vasthai said.

James and Chris looked at each with the look of disbelief. They were stuck between a rock and a hard place. "Vas...,"before her name could come from James' mouth a silent bullet was fired at him, barely missing his arm.

Although, they didn't hear the gun fire they heard the bullet when it hit the ground. When they realized that they were not fucking around; James and Chris started shedding their clothes.

The next command came from Tyrone. The last twenty four hours had been unreal for him. He had been exposed to a lot of information that he had no idea about. Now he was standing with his parents seeking the retribution that he was plotting against the man who had given him the gene to be a rapist.

"Yo, pops I got something real special for you!!! Since you enjoy taking people's innocence, let me see how well you take it when yours is violated. Simon Says Chris you bend James over

and fuck him like he was your bitch!!"Tyrone said as the entire circle began to laugh.

James was petrified. One of things that he was most against was homosexuality. "Man, fuck this and fuck you, if you think I'm about to bend over and let this nigga fuck me!!! Y'all need to go ahead and pull them triggers!!" He said.

Tyrone looked at him and without even acknowledging him the bullet hit his leg causing him to fall to the ground. He screamed from the pain as he grabbed his leg trying to stop the bleeding.

"Now, fuck that nigga!!! I swear the next bullet will be to your dome!!!" Tyrone yelled at Chris.

Chris was not into that gay shit either, but he was stuck. He had no choice in this matter. He was on survival mode and he was trying to spare his life by all means necessary. Chris pulled at his dick in an attempt to get it hard. The act of the pulling stimulated him mildly and he entered James' ass rough and with force.

James let out the most horrific moan that was ever heard by man. Not only was he in pain from the bullet wound, but, also from the pain coming from his asshole.

Vasthai laughed the loudest because she thought how poetic this moment was. She told James that she was going to fuck him until he bled and now she was watching the shit in living color.

The circle had gone around until it reached Kennedy. She had been waiting on this moment, the moment that she was able to face the man who was

her father. Tears wailed in her eyes as she said, "James, Simon Says repeat after me. I raped my sister and now you look at your daughter/niece."

James could not comprehend what he had just heard. He was wounded from the words and as his eyes met the child that he had fathered with his sister a gunshot hit him in the arm.

Phoenix's gun had fired the blow. She had all intentions of inflicting as much pain and humiliation as possible. She walked directly to where her brother was and stooped down on the ground so that she could see his eyes. When their eyes met Phoenix stared deep into them, searching for his soul.

Phoenix was disgusted by what she saw within his eyes. She looked at him and said, "Oh you shocked that you knocked me up!!!? Don't be. You came into my room and you fucked me! Your lil'sister. The one who looked up to you and wanted to be just like you!!! You changed me from confident to ashamed all in one night!!!" Phoenix had faced her demon and now she was ready to put an end to her life of disappointments.

She turned around and faced her daughter. The tears that were in her eyes clouded her vision. Phoenix couldn't see the sun from the trees.

"Kennedy, this was never your fault. I tried the best I could with what I had. Forgive me." Her soul was on display for all to see.

Phoenix was tired of being among the living. Although, she had been clean and she and Kennedy had the chance to reconnect as mother and daughter, the shame of what happened to her was a burden

that she could not move on from.

For the first time Kennedy felt as if she could move on from the stigma of being an incest victim. She forgave her mother and was ready to mend the shattered pieces of their mother/daughter relationship.

All eyes were on Kennedy as she took two steps forward to embrace her mother, but as she was walking closer to her mother Phoenix had taken out a needle filled with heroin. This was going to be her first and last time trying this addictive drug.

The dope that was in the needle was almost pure. Phoenix was seeking that everlasting high. The night's dark concealed Phoenix as she tied the belt around her arm and pulled tight enough for her vein to be exposed.

Kennedy walked slowly, but when she came close enough to her mother she saw what she was about to do. Without saying a word she ran in the direction of Phoenix, but Kennedy's eyes saw her mother fall to the ground as she reached her.

The sounds of shock escaped all of their mouths. As Tyrone and Patrick continued to hold James and Chris at gunpoint, the women tended to Phoenix. They watched her body convulse in seizures. The foam from her mouth fell on the sides of her face. She had been drug free for thirty days and had waited for this night to kill herself.

Vasthai looked at Kennedy and said, "Let's do this nigga!! He is the reason why she no longer wanted to fight!" The two women locked eyes and instantly their minds were in tune with each other.

They both grabbed their silenced guns and

took aim at James and Chris. As they were about to pull the trigger, the sound of an approaching vehicle could be heard coming toward them. All eyes were on the van that had found them deep in the woods.

"Everyone chill. This is our ride!!! Oh boys, I have one more surprise for you before I dome the both of you!!!" Vasthai said with her gun pointing at them, while never taking her eyes from either James or Chris.

The silhouette of a woman could be seen from the light of the moon. The woman approached the group and was directly in front for all to see.

Tyrone, James and Chris' mouths were open from shock. "What the fuck!! Why is the warden here?" Tyrone said, as he pointed his gun in her direction.

The warden looked at Tyrone and replied, "I see your mother has not told you yet." Tyrone along with the others was confused. They had no idea what was going on.

Vasthai knew that she needed to regain control of the situation, "Tyrone, I want you to meet my mother…your grandmother. Do you think you were sent to Yazoo City prison randomly? Your grandmother requested that your time be served in her prison so she could make sure that you were safe." She said.

Kaori and her daughter had reconnected after Vasthai learned why Tyrone was requested to serve his time at the Yazoo prison. Kaori explained to Vasthai the reason why she was not in her life and begged for forgiveness.

It was from that point on that Kaori had made a vow that she was going to be there for her daughter and when Vasthai came to her with her plan to kill the men who raped her Kaori was down for the cause. When the door of Vasthai's painful past was fully closed she and Vasthai would be able to start anew.

Tyrone was in total disbelief. He could not believe that his grandmother was the warden. As Tyrone was thinking on all that had happened; Chris saw that he was slipping, and made the executive decision to make a play for the gun. Chris looked around and saw his opportunity.

Chris stepped quickly and managed to catch Tyrone off guard. There was a struggle and the gun fell to the ground. As Chris crawled to the gun he was stopped in his tracks as Layce shot him at close range in his head.

Layce had just become a cold-blooded killer in a matter of seconds. When she read Vasthai's instructions that were hand delivered to her she also received Chris' DNA semen results. They showed that he was 99.99% match to the semen found in Vasthai's rape kit.

After reading and seeing the evidence Layce confronted Chris and he never confirmed or denied the accusation. It was then that she knew that she was not going to spend the rest of her life with him, but instead be his judge and jury.

She stepped over his lifeless body and picked up the gun and handed it back to Tyrone. Tyrone pulled himself together and got up from the ground taking the gun from Layce. He looked down

at Chris and saw that he was dead. James was the lone survivor and he knew that he was next to die.

He was so weak and his mind was spiraling in a world of confusion. In less than twenty-four hours James had learned that he fathered his sister's child, he was going to be murdered, and that the warden of the prison where he worked was the mother of the woman who he raped many years ago.

James also just witnessed his sister kill herself without him ever telling her that he was sorry for what he did. He was ready to go. If death and Hell was coming his way, he was ready to die... it was better than sitting there being tortured and belittled.

With the little bit of energy James had left he was able to pull himself off of the ground and he stood before his enemies. He was naked as the day he had come into the world as he stood there waiting for the bullet to come.

"What the fuck are y'all waiting for!!!? Let's get this shit over with!!!" He told them.

Vasthai knew that time was of the essence. "Let's do this nigga!!! Mom can you and Tyrone go get the boat. Patrick, help me to drag Chris' body over here. Kennedy you keep your gun on this mutha'fucker. If he blinks...you rock this nigga's dome!!!" Vasthai quickly called off her demands as she and Patrick walked over to get Chris' lifeless corpse.

It was Kennedy and her father standing face to face for the first time in her life. She was feeling trigger happy and was waiting for him to give her a reason to blast his ass.

Kennedy needed to tell him a few words. "You are a sorry excuse for a fucking human being!!! You fuck up everyone who you have ever come in contact with. I am so ready to off you that I want to shit on you and let you feel how it feels to be shitted on!!" She said to him as she stepped directly in his face. They were head to head and eye to eye.

James was at a lost for words. What could he say that would change his current circumstance and erase the pain of the past? Every word that she uttered from her lips to his ears was nothing but the truth. At this point he was too defeated to fight back so he stood and took the verbal abuse.

Kaori and Layce returned to where Kennedy stood with a small 15ft all purpose fishing boat in tow. Vasthai and Patrick dragged Chris over to the boat. Once they were all together they knew the plan and began to work to finish the job.

As everyone was doing their part Vasthai walked over to Kennedy and pulled her to the side. "Look, I am sorry about your mom, but you know that we can't leave her out here. You know that we are going to have to dispose of her body." She explained to her.

Kennedy was quite aware of what she was telling her. Although, she had never been close to her mother because of the drugs and incest, she now knew that she was free of her heartache and pain.

"I know. I just wished that we had more time. Since we are family now by Tyrone being my brother we all have to stick together." Kennedy said, as she walked back over, helping the others.

Vasthai walked back over slowly to where everyone was. She had never even thought about it until Kennedy mentioned it...she was right. Kennedy and Tyrone were in fact brother and sister.

When it was all said and done James and Chris' corpse were tied together facing away from each other. Their hands and legs were handcuffed to each other to ensure that it was a death of togetherness. "

"Do you have any last words?" Layce asked him.

James looked at her and said, "I will see you in hell...BITCH!" Layce looked at him and laughed. Layce spit on her husband and turned her back to him.

When she walked away, Kennedy came squatted directly in his face, and pissed and shitted. Then she wiped her ass and threw the tissue on him. When it was Patrick and Tyrone's turn they both pulled out their dicks and pissed on James and Chris.

It was now Vasthai's turned to say goodbye. She turned James over so that Chris' body was visible. She pulled out the razor that she had in her pants pocket and severed his dick and balls.

As soon as the organ was removed from his body, his body drained itself of his blood. Vasthai turned Chris back over until he was no longer on top and James was now facing them. Vasthai said no words. With her gun she opened his mouth and with her free hand placed the dick in it.

There was silence among them as they began to hear hissing coming from the water that was directly behind. The wildlife smelled the blood of their prey. Kaori pulled the boat in the front as Vasthai, Patrick, and Tyrone pushed the boat from behind. They made it to the edge of the water and pushed the boat into it.

The boat drifted slowly into the center of the swamp. Then the sound of the hissing became louder and more prominent. Suddenly, they all saw the alligator emerge from the water and attack the boat.

The sounds of the animal eating James and Chris' flesh was like hearing meat going through a meat grinder. True, it was a horrendous way to die and a sure way to discard the evidence of a murder.

When the boat was completed submerged in the water, they laid Phoenix's body in the water and waited for the gators to again appear.

The six people cleaned up the crime scene, got back on the bus, and headed back to Yazoo City. They stopped twenty miles outside of the city limits abandoning the jail bus and picking up their vehicles.

They all got into their cars and headed toward the interstate going their separate ways...to start their lives.

Epilogue

Vasthai was sitting in her weekly counseling session with her psychologist Rodney. It had been a year since she took care of her issue with her past.

Although, she would never come out and tell him the crime she committed, Rodney knew what she had done.

He had learned his lesson and he would never again risk his livelihood again by breaking the doctor/patient confidentiality clause.

"Vasthai, your homework for this week is for you to write a letter to yourself and express all of the emotions that you are feeling. When you have finished it throw it away and forgive yourself and move on." Rodney told her, as he walked her to the door.

A week later Vasthai sat at her desk in her private home office. She picked up a notepad, a pen, and began to write her letter to herself.

Dear Vasthai,

How do you begin to heal from a past that has been drenched in nothing but pain and heartache? You have been through many trials and tribulations and you still managed to come out on top. You have lied, manipulated, and killed to escape your past, but now it is time to move on!! It will take time to heal, but I know with God's guidance and your family you can make it. Know

that you are a good person. You were able to free yourself and others from the same pain caused by the man who raped you. Now make this your last time mentioning or thinking about this burden that has already been lifted from you!! Know that you are loved and that is all that matters. Make the best of what you have and want for nothing.
Signed,
Damaged Goods

Also by Nikki Urban